Brander Matthews

Tales of Fantasy and Fact

Brander Matthews

Tales of Fantasy and Fact

ISBN/EAN: 9783337072506

Printed in Europe, USA, Canada, Australia, Japan

Cover: Foto ©Andreas Hilbeck / pixelio.de

More available books at **www.hansebooks.com**

TALES OF FANTASY AND FACT

BY

BRANDER MATTHEWS

NEW YORK
HARPER & BROTHERS PUBLISHERS
1896

BOOKS BY BRANDER MATTHEWS.

THE THEATRES OF PARIS.
FRENCH DRAMATISTS OF THE 19TH CENTURY.
THE LAST MEETING, a Story.
A SECRET OF THE SEA, and Other Stories.
PEN AND INK: Essays on Subjects of More or Less Importance.
A FAMILY TREE, and Other Stories.
WITH MY FRIENDS: Tales Told in Partnership.
A TALE OF TWENTY-FIVE HOURS.
TOM PAULDING, a Story for Boys.
IN THE VESTIBULE LIMITED, a Story.
AMERICANISMS AND BRITICISMS, with Other Essays on Other Isms.
THE STORY OF A STORY, and Other Stories.
THE DECISION OF THE COURT, a Comedy.
STUDIES OF THE STAGE.
THIS PICTURE AND THAT, a Comedy.
VIGNETTES OF MANHATTAN.
THE ROYAL MARINE, an Idyl of Narragansett.
BOOK-BINDINGS, Old and New; Notes of a Book-Lover.
HIS FATHER'S SON, a Novel of New York.
AN INTRODUCTION TO THE STUDY OF AMERICAN LITERA-
    TURE.
TALES OF FANTASY AND FACT.
ASPECTS OF FICTION, and Other Ventures in Criticism. (*In Press.*)

TO

THE MEMORY OF MY FRIEND

H. C. BUNNER

CONTENTS

A PRIMER OF IMAGINARY
GEOGRAPHY

A PRIMER OF IMAGINARY
GEOGRAPHY

"**S**HIP ahoy!"

There was an answer from our bark—for such it seemed to me by this time—but I could not make out the words.

"Where do you hail from?" was the next question.

I strained my ears to catch the response, being naturally anxious to know whence I had come.

"From the City of Destruction!" was what I thought I heard; and I confess that it surprised me not a little.

"Where are you bound?" was asked in turn.

Again I listened with intensest interest, and again did the reply astonish me greatly.

"Ultima Thule!" was the answer from our boat, and the voice of the man who answered was deep and melancholy.

Then I knew that I had set out strange countries for to see, and that I was all un-equipped for so distant a voyage. Thule I knew, or at least I had heard of the king who reigned there once and who cast his goblet into the sea. But Ultima Thule! was not that beyond the uttermost borders of the earth?

"Any passengers?" was the next query, and I noted that the voice came now from the left and was almost abreast of us.

"One only," responded the captain of our boat.

"Where bound?" was the final inquiry.

"To the Fortunate Islands!" was the an-swer; and as I heard this my spirits rose again, and I was glad, as what man would not be who was on his way to the paradise where the crimson-flowered meadows are full of the shade of frankincense-trees and of fruits of gold?

Then the boat bounded forward again, and I heard the wash of the waves.

All this time it seemed as though I were in

darkness; but now I began dimly to discern the objects about me. I found that I was lying on a settee in a state-room at the stern of the vessel. Through the small round window over my head the first rays of the rising sun darted and soon lighted the little cabin.

As I looked about me with curiosity, wondering how I came to be a passenger on so unexpected a voyage, I saw the figure of a man framed in the doorway at the foot of the stairs leading to the deck above.

How it was I do not know, but I made sure at once that he was the captain of the ship, the man whose voice I had heard answering the hail.

He was tall and dark, with a scant beard and a fiery and piercing gaze, which penetrated me as I faced him. Yet the expression of his countenance was not unfriendly; nor could any man lay eyes upon him without a movement of pity for the sadness written on his visage.

I rose to my feet as he came forward.

"Well," he said, holding out his hand, "and how are you after your nap?"

He spoke our language with ease and yet

with a foreign accent. Perhaps it was this which betrayed him to me.

"Are you not Captain Vanderdecken?" I asked as I took his hand heartily.

"So you know me?" he returned, with a mournful little laugh, as he motioned to me to sit down again.

Thus the ice was broken, and he took his seat by my side, and we were soon deep in talk.

When he learned that I was a loyal New-Yorker, his cordiality increased.

"I have relatives in New Amsterdam," he cried; "at least I had once. Diedrich Knickerbocker was my first cousin. And do you know Rip Van Winkle?"

Although I could not claim any close friendship with this gentleman, I boasted myself fully acquainted with his history.

"Yes, yes," said Captain Vanderdecken, "I suppose he was before your time. Most people are so short-lived nowadays; it's only with that Wandering Jew now that I ever have a chat over old times. Well, well, but you have heard of Rip? Were you ever told that I was on a visit to Hendrik Hudson the night Rip went up the mountain and took a drop too much ?"

I had to confess that here was a fact I had not before known.

"I ran up the river," said the Hollander, "to have a game of bowls with the Englishman and his crew, nearly all of them countrymen of mine; and, by-the-way, Hudson always insists that it was I who brought the storm with me that gave poor Rip Van Winkle the rheumatism as he slept off his intoxication on the hillside under the pines. He was a good fellow, Rip, and a very good judge of schnapps, too."

Seeing him smile with the pleasant memories of past companionship, I marvelled when the sorrowful expression swiftly covered his face again as a mask.

"But why talk of those who are dead and gone and are happy?" he asked in his deep voice. "Soon there will be no one left, perhaps, but Ahasuerus and Vanderdecken—the Wandering Jew and the Flying Dutchman."

He sighed bitterly, and then he gave a short, hard laugh.

"There's no use talking about these things, is there?" he cried. "In an hour or two, if the wind holds, I can show you the house in which Ahasuerus has established his museum, the only solace of his lonely life. He has the most extraordinary gathering of curiosities the world has ever seen—truly a virtuoso's collection. An American reporter came on a voyage with me fifty or sixty years ago, and I took him over there. His name was Hawthorne. He interviewed the Jew, and wrote up the collection in the American papers, so I've been told."

"I remember reading the interview," I said, "and it was indeed a most remarkable collection."

"It's all the more curious now for the odds and ends I've been able to pick up here and there for my old friend," Vanderdecken declared; "I got him the horn of Hernani, the harpoon with which Long Tom Coffin pinned the British officer to the mast, the long rifle of Natty Bumppo, the letter A in scarlet cloth embroidered in gold by Hester Prynne, the banner with the strange device 'Excelsior,' the gold bug which was once used as a plummet,

Maud Muller's rake, and the jack-knives of Hosea Biglow and Sam Lawson."

"You must have seen extraordinary things yourself," I ventured to suggest.

" No man has seen stranger," he answered, promptly. "No man has ever been witness to more marvellous deeds than I—not even Ahasuerus, I verily believe, for he has only the land, and I have the boundless sea. I survey mankind from China to Peru. I have heard the horns of elfland blowing, and I could tell you the song the sirens sang. I have dropped anchor at the No Man's Land, and off Lyonesse, and in Xanadu, where Alph the sacred river ran. I have sailed from the still-vexed Bermoothes to the New Atlantis, of which there is no mention even until the year 1629."

" In which year there was published an account of it written in the Latin tongue, but by an Englishman," I said, desirous to reveal my acquirements.

"I have seen every strange coast," continued the Flying Dutchman. " The Island of Bells and Robinson Crusoe's Island and the Kingdoms of Brobdingnag and Lilliput. But it is not for me to vaunt myself for my voyages. And of a truth there are men I should like to have met and talked with whom I have yet failed to see. Especially is there one Ulysses, a sailor-man of antiquity who called himself Outis, whence I have sometimes suspected that he came from the town of Weissnicht-wo."

Just to discover what Vanderdecken would say, I inquired innocently whether this was the same person as one Captain Nemo of whose submarine exploits I had read.

"Captain Nemo?" the Flying Dutchman repeated scornfully. "I never heard of him. Are you sure there is such a fellow?"

I tried to turn the conversation by asking if he had ever met another ancient mariner named Charon.

"Oh, yes," was his answer. "Charon keeps the ferry across the Styx to the Elysian Fields, past the sunless marsh of Acheron. Yes—I've met him more than once. I met him only last month, and he was very proud of his new electric launch with its storage battery."

When I expressed my surprise at this, he asked me if I did not know that the under-

world was now lighted by electricity, and that
Pluto had put in all the modern improvements. Before I had time to answer, he
rose from his seat and slapped me on the
shoulder.

"Come up with me!—if you want to behold
things for yourself," he cried. "So far, it
seems to me, you have never seen the sights!"

I followed him on deck. The sun was now
two hours high, and I could just make out a
faint line of land on the horizon.

"That rugged coast is Bohemia, which is
really a desert country by the sea, although ignorant and bigoted pedants have dared to deny
it," and the scorn of my companion as he said
this was wonderful to see. "Its borders touch
Alsatia, of which the chief town is a city of ref-
uge. Not far inland, but a little to the south,
is the beautiful Forest of Arden, where men
and maids dwell together in amity, and where
clowns wander, making love to shepherdesses.
Some of these same pestilent pedants have pretended to believe that this forest of Arden was
situated in France, which is absurd, as there
are no serpents and no lions in France, while
we have the best of evidence as to the exist-

ence of both in Arden—you know that, don't you?"

I admitted that a green and gilded snake and a lioness with udders all drawn dry were known to have been seen there both on the same day. I ventured to suggest further that possibly this Forest of Arden was the Wandering Wood where Una met her lion.

"Of course," was the curt response; "everybody knows that Arden is a most beautiful region; even the toads there have precious jewels in their heads. And if you range the forest freely you may chance to find also the White Doe of Rylstone and the goat with the gilded horns that told fortunes in Paris long ago by tapping with his hoof on a tambourine."

"These, then, are the Happy Hunting-Grounds?" I suggested with a light laugh.

"Who would chase a tame goat?" he retorted with ill-concealed contempt for my ill-advised remark.

I thought it best to keep silence; and after a minute or two he resumed the conversation, like one who is glad of a good listener.

"In the outskirts of the Forest of Arden," he began again, "stands the Abbey of Thelema — the only abbey which is bounded by no wall and in which there is no clock at all nor any dial.   And what need is there of knowing the time when one has for companions only comely and well - conditioned men and fair women of sweet disposition?   And the motto of the Abbey of Thelema is *Fais ce que voudra* — Do what you will; and many of those who dwell in the Forest of Arden will tell you that they have taken this also for their device, and that if you live under the greenwood tree you may spend your life—as you like it."

I acknowledged that this claim was probably well founded, since I recalled a song of the foresters in which they declared themselves without an enemy but winter and rough weather.

" Yes," he went on, " they are fond of singing in the Forest of Arden, and they sing good songs.   And so they do in the fair land beyond where I have never been, and which I can never hope to go to see for myself, if all that they report be true—and yet what would I not give to see it and to die there."

And as he said this sadly, his voice sank into a sigh.

"And where does the road through the forest lead, that you so much wish to set forth upon it?" I asked.

"That's the way to Arcady," he said—"to Arcady where all the leaves are merry. I may not go there, though I long for it. Those who attain to its borders never come back again—and why should they leave it? Yet there are tales told, and I have heard that this Arcady is the veritable El Dorado, and that in it is the true Fountain of Youth, gushing forth unfailingly for the refreshment of all who may reach it. But no one may find the entrance who cannot see it by the light that never was on land or sea."

"It must be a favored region," I remarked.

"Of a truth it is," he answered; "and on the way there is the orchard where grow the golden apples of Hesperides, and the dragon is dead now that used to guard them, and so any one may help himself to the beautiful fruit. And by the side of the orchard flows the river Lethe, of which it is not well for man to drink, though many men would taste it gladly." And again he sighed.

I knew not what to say, and so waited for him to speak once more.

"That promontory there on the weather bow," he began again after a few moments' silence, "that is Barataria, which was long supposed to be an island by its former governor, Don Sancho Panza, but which is now known by all to be connected with the mainland. Pleasant pastures slope down to the water, and if we were closer in shore you might chance to see Rozinante, the famous charger of Don Quixote de la Mancha, grazing amicably with the horse that brought the good news from Ghent to Aix."

"I wish I could see them!" I cried, enthusiastically; "but there is another horse I would rather behold than any — the winged steed Pegasus."

Before responding, my guide raised his hand and shaded his eyes and scanned the horizon.

"No," he said at last. "I cannot descry any this afternoon. Sometimes in these latitudes I have seen a dozen hippogriffs circling about the ship, and I should like to have shown them to you. Perhaps they are all in the paddock at the stock-farm, where Apollo is now mating them with night-mares in the hope of improving the breed from which he selects the coursers that draw the chariot of the sun. They say that the experiment would have more chance of success if it were easier to find the night-mares' nests."

"It was not a hippogriff I desired to see especially," I returned when he paused, "although that would be interesting, no doubt. It was the renowned Pegasus himself."

"Pegasus is much like the other hippogriffs," he retorted, "although perhaps he has a little better record than any of them. But they say he has not won a single aërial handicap since that American professor of yours harnessed him to a one-hoss shay. That seemed to break his spirit, somehow; and I'm told he would shy now even at a broomstick train."

"Even if he is out of condition," I declared, "Pegasus is still the steed I desire to see above all."

"I haven't set eyes on him for weeks," was the answer, "so he is probably moulting; this is the time of year. He has a roomy boxstall in the new Augean stable at the foot of Mount Parnassus. You know they have turned the

spring of Castaly so that it flows through the
stable-yard now, and so it is easy enough to
keep the place clean."

"If I may not see Pegasus," I asked, "is
there any chance of my being taken to the
Castle of the Sleeping Beauty?"

"I have never seen it myself," he replied,
"and so I cannot show it to you. Rarely indeed may I leave the deck of my ship to go
ashore ; and this castle that you ask about is
very far inland. I am told that it is in a
country which the French travellers call *La
Scribie*, a curious land, wherein the scene is
laid of many a play, because its laws and its
customs are exactly what every playwright
has need of ; but no poet has visited it for
many years. Yet the Grand Duchess of Ger-
olstein, whose domains lie partly within the
boundaries of Scribia, is still a subscriber to
the *Gazette de Hollande*—the only newspaper
I take himself, by the way."

This last remark of the Captain's explained
how it was that he had been able to keep up
with the news of the day, despite his constant
wanderings over the waste of waters ; and
what more natural in fact than that the Flying

Dutchman should be a regular reader of the *Holland Gazette?*

Vanderdecken went forward into the prow of the vessel, calling to me to follow.

"Do you see those peaks afar in the distance?" he asked, pointing over the starboard bow.

I could just make out a saw-like outline in the direction indicated.

"Those are the Delectable Mountains," he informed me; "and down in a hollow between the two ranges is the Happy Valley."

"Where Rasselas lived?"

"Yes," he replied, "and beyond the Delectable Mountains, on the far slope, lies Prester John's Kingdom, and there dwell anthropophagi, and men whose heads do grow beneath their shoulders. At least, so they say. For my part, I have never seen any such. And I have now no desire to go to Prester John's Kingdom, since I have been told that he has lately married Pope Joan. Do you see that grove of trees there at the base of the mountains?"

I answered that I thought I could distinguish weirdly contorted branches and strangely shivering foliage.

"That is the deadly upas-tree," he explained, "and it is as much as a man's life is worth to lie down in the shade of its twisted limbs. I slept there, on that point where the trees are the thickest, for a fortnight a century or so ago—but all I had for my pains was a headache. Still I should not advise you to adventure yourself under the shadow of those melancholy boughs."

I confess at once that I was little prompted to a visit so dangerous and so profitless.

"Profitless?" he repeated. "As to that I am not so certain, for if you have a mind to see the rarest animals in the world, you could there sate your curiosity. On the shore, between the foot-hills and the grove of upas, is a park of wild beasts, the like of which no man has looked upon elsewhere. Even from the deck of this ship I have seen more than once a drove of unicorns, or a herd of centaurs, come down to the water to drink; and sometimes I have caught a pleasant glimpse of satyrs and fauns dancing in the sunlight. And once indeed—I shall never forget that extraordinary spectacle—as I sped past with every sail set and a ten-knot breeze astern, I saw the phœnix

blaze up in its new birth, while the little sala-
manders frisked in the intense flame."

"The phœnix?" I cried. "You have seen
the phœnix?"

"In just this latitude," he answered, "but it
was about nine o'clock in the evening and I
remember that the new moon was setting
behind the mountains when I happened to
come on deck."

"And what was the phœnix like?" I asked.

"Really," he replied, "the bird was almost
as Herodotus described her, of the make and
size of the eagle, with a plumage partly red
and partly golden. If we go by the point by
noon, perhaps you may see her for yourself."

"Is she there still?" I asked, in wonder.

"Why not?" he returned. "All the game of
this sort is carefully preserved and the law is
off on phœnixes only once in a century. Why,
if it were not for the keepers, there soon would
not be a single griffin or dragon left, not a
single sphinx, not a single chimæra. Even as
it is, I am told they do not breed as freely
now as when they could roam the whole world
in safety. That is why the game laws are so
rigorous. Indeed, I am informed and believe

that it is not permitted to kill the were-wolves even when their howling, as they run at large at night, prevents all sleep. It is true, of course, that very few people care to remain in such a neighborhood."

"I should think not," I agreed. "And what manner of people are they who dare to live here?"

"Along the shore there are a few harpies," he answered; "and now and then I have seen a mermaid on the rocks combing her hair with a golden comb as she sang to herself."

"Harpies?" I repeated, in disgust. "Why not the sea-serpent also?"

"There was a sea-serpent which lived for years in that cove yonder," said the Captain, pointing to a pleasant bay on the starboard, "but I have not seen it lately. Unless I am in error, it had a pitched battle hereabouts with a kraken. I don't remember who got the better of the fight —but I haven't seen the snake since."

As I scanned the surface of the water to see if I might not detect some trace of one or another of these marvellous beasts of the sea, I remarked a bank of fog lying across our course.

"And what is this that we are coming to?" I inquired.

"That?" Captain Vanderdecken responded, indicating the misty outline straight before us. "That is Altruria—at least it is so down in the charts, but I have never set eyes on it actually. It belongs to Utopia, you know; and they say that, although it is now on the level of the earth, it used once to be a flying island—the same which was formerly known as Laputa, and which was first visited and described by Captain Lemuel Gulliver about the year 1727, or a little earlier."

"So that is Altruria," I said, trying in vain to see it more clearly. "There was an Altrurian in New York not long ago, but I had no chance of speech with him."

"They are pleasant folk, those Altrurians," said the Captain, "although rather given to boasting. And they have really little enough to brag about, after all. Their climate is execrable—I find it ever windy hereabouts, and when I get in sight of that bank of fog, I always look out for squalls. I don't know just what the population is now, but I doubt if it is growing. You see, people talk about moving there to live, but they are rarely in a hurry to do it, I notice. Nor are the manufactures of the Altrurians as many as they were said to be. Their chief export now is the famous Procrustean bed; although the old house of Damocles & Co. still does a good business in swords. Their tonnage is not what it used to be, and I'm told that they are issuing a good deal of paper money now to try and keep the balance of trade in their favor."

"Are there not many poets among the inhabitants of Altruria?" I asked.

"They are all poets and romancers of one kind or another," declared the Captain. "Come below again into the cabin, and I will show you some of their books."

The sky was now overcast and there was a chill wind blowing, so I was not at all loath to leave the deck, and to follow Vanderdecken down the steps into the cabin.

He took a thin volume from the table. "This," he said, is one of their books—'News from Nowhere,' it is called."

He extended it towards me, and I held out my hand for it, but it slipped through my fingers. I started forward in a vain effort to seize it.

As I did so, the walls and the floor of the cabin seemed to melt away and to dissolve in air, and beyond them and taking their place were the walls and floor of my own house. Then suddenly the clock on the mantelpiece struck five, and I heard a bob-tail car rattling and clattering past the door on its way across town to Union Square, and thence to Greenwich Village, and so on down to the Hoboken Ferry.

Then I found myself on my own sofa, bending forward to pick up the volume of Cyrano de Bergerac, which lay on the carpet at my feet. I sat up erect and collected my thoughts as best I could after so strange a journey. And I wondered why it was that no one had ever prepared a primer of imaginary geography, giving to airy nothings a local habitation and a name, and accompanying it with an atlas of maps in the manner of the *Carte du Pays de Tendre.*

(1894.)

THE KINETOSCOPE OF TIME

THE KINETOSCOPE OF TIME

S the twelfth stroke of the bell in the tower at the corner tolled forth slowly, the midnight wind blew chill down the deserted avenue, and swept it clear of all belated wayfarers. The bare trees in the thin strip of park clashed their lifeless branches; the river far below slipped along silently. There was no moon, and the stars were shrouded. It was a black night. Yet far in the distance there was a gleam of cheerful light which lured me on and on. I could not have said why it was that I had ventured forth at that hour on such a night. It seemed to me as though the yellow glimmer I beheld afar off was the goal of my excursion. Something within whispered to me then that I need go no farther when once I had come to the spot whence the soft glare proceeded.

The pall of darkness was so dense that I could not see the sparse houses I chanced to pass, nor did I know where I was any more. I urged forward blindly, walking towards the light, which was all that broke the blackness before me; its faint illumination seemed to me somehow to be kindly, inviting, irresistible. At last I came to a halt in front of a building I had never before seen, although I thought myself well acquainted with that part of the city. It was a circular edifice, or so it seemed to me then; and I judged that it had but a single story, or two, at the most. The door stood open to the street; and it was from this that the light was cast. So dim was this illumination now I had come to it that I marvelled I could have seen it at all afar off as I was when first I caught sight of it.

While I stood at the portal of the unsuspected edifice, peering doubtfully within, wondering to what end I had been led thither, and hesitating as to my next step, I felt again the impulse to go forward. At that moment tiny darts of fire, as it were, glowed at the end of

the hall that opened before me, and they ran
together rapidly and joined in liquid lines and
then faded as suddenly as they had come—
but not too soon for me to read the simple
legend they had written in the air—an invi-
tation to me, so I interpreted it, to go forward
again, to enter the building, and to see for
myself why I had been enticed there.

Without hesitation I obeyed.   I walked
through the doorway, and I became conscious that the door had closed behind me as
I pressed forward.   The passage was narrow
and but faintly lighted; it bent to the right
with a circular sweep as though it skirted the
inner circumference of the building; still curv-
ing, it sank by a gentle gradient; and then it
rose again and turned almost at right angles.
Pushing ahead resolutely, although in not a
little doubt as to the meaning of my adventure, I thrust aside a heavy curtain, soft to the
hand.   Then I found myself just inside a large
circular hall.   Letting the hangings fall behind me, I took three or four irresolute paces
which brought me almost to the centre of the
room.   I saw that the walls were continuously
draped with the heavy folds of the same soft

velvet, so that I could not even guess where it was I had entered. The rotunda was bare of all furniture; there was no table in it, no chair, no sofa; nor was anything hanging from the ceiling or against the curtained walls. All that the room contained was a set of four curiously shaped narrow stands, placed over against one another at the corners of what might be a square drawn within the circle of the hall. These narrow stands were close to the curtains; they were perhaps a foot wide, each of them, or it might be a little more: they were twice or three times as long as they were wide; and they reached a height of possibly three or four feet.

Going towards one of these stands to examine it more curiously, I discovered that there were two projections from the top, resembling eye-pieces, as though inviting the beholder to gaze into the inside of the stand. Then I thought I heard a faint metallic click above my head. Raising my eyes swiftly, I read a few words written, as it were, against the dark velvet of the heavy curtains in dots of flame that flowed one into the other and melted away in a moment. When this mysterious legend had

faded absolutely, I could not recall the words
I had read in the fitful and flitting letters of
fire, and yet I retained the meaning of the
message; and I understood that if I chose to
peer through the eye-pieces I should see a
succession of strange dances.

To gaze upon dancing was not what I had
gone forth to do, but I saw no reason why I
should not do so, as I was thus strangely bid-
den. I lowered my head until my eyes were
close to the two openings at the top of the
stand. I looked into blackness at first, and
yet I thought that I could detect a mystic
commotion of the invisible particles at which
I was staring. I made no doubt that, if I
waited, in due season the promise would be
fulfilled. After a period of expectancy which
I could not measure, infinitesimal sparks darted hither and thither, and there was a slight
crackling sound. I concentrated my attention on what I was about to see; and in a
moment more I was rewarded.

The darkness took shape and robed itself in
color; and there arose out of it a spacious
banquet-hall, where many guests sat at supper.
I could not make out whether they were Ro-

mans or Orientals; the structure itself had a
Latin solidity, but the decorations were Eastern
in their glowing gorgeousness. The hall was
illumined by hanging lamps, by the light of
which I tried to decide whether the ruler who
sat in the seat of honor was a Roman or an
Oriental. The beautiful woman beside him
struck me as Eastern beyond all question.
While I gazed intently he turned to her and
proffered a request. She smiled acquiescence,
and there was a flash of anticipated triumph
in her eye as she beckoned to a menial and
sent him forth with a message. A movement
as of expectancy ran around the tables where
the guests sat at meat. The attendants opened
wide the portals and a young girl came forward. She was perhaps fourteen or fifteen
years of age, but in the East women ripen
young, and her beauty was indisputable. She
had large, deep eyes and a full mouth; and
there was a chain of silver and golden coins
twisted into her coppery hair. She was so like
to the woman who sat beside the ruler that I
did not doubt them to be mother and daughter. At a word from the elder the younger
began to dance; and her dance was Oriental,

slow at first, but holding every eye with its
sensual fascination. The girl was a mistress
of the art; and not a man in the room withdrew his gaze from her till she made an end
and stood motionless before the ruler. He
said a few words I could not hear, and then
the daughter turned to the mother for guid-
ance; and again I caught the flash of triumph
in the elder woman's eye and on her face the
suggestion of a hatred about to be glutted.
And then the light faded and the darkness
settled down on the scene and I saw no more.

I did not raise my head from the stand, for
I felt sure that this was not all I was to behold; and in a few moments there was again
a faint scintillation. In time the light was
strong enough for me to perceive the irregular
flames of a huge bonfire burning in an old
square of some mediæval city. It was evening, and yet a throng of men and women and
children made an oval about the fire and about
a slim girl who had spread a Persian carpet on
the rough stones of the broad street. She was
a brunette, with dense black hair; she wore a
striped skirt, and a jacket braided with gold
had slipped from her bare shoulders. She held

a tambourine in her hand and she was twisting and turning in cadence to her own song.
Then she went to one side where stood a white
goat with gilded horns and put down her tambourine and took up two swords; and with
these in her hands she resumed her dance. A
man in the throng, a man of scant thirty-five,
but already bald, a man of stalwart frame,
fixed hot eyes upon her; and from time to
time a smile and a sigh met on his lips, but
the smile was more dolorous than the sigh.
And as the gypsy girl ceased her joyous gyrations, the bonfire died out, and darkness fell
on the scene again, and I could no longer see
anything.

Again I waited, and after an interval no
longer than the other there came a faint glow
that grew until I saw clearly as in the morning sun the glade of a forest through which a
brook rippled. A sad-faced woman sat on a
stone by the side of the streamlet; her gray
garments set off the strange ornament in the
fashion of a single letter of the alphabet that
was embroidered in gold and in scarlet over
her heart. Visible at some distance was a little girl, like a bright - apparelled vision, in a

sunbeam, which fell down upon her through
an arch of boughs. The ray quivered to and
fro, making her figure dim or distinct, now
like a real child, now like a child's spirit, as the
splendor came and went. With violets and
anemones and columbines the little girl had
decorated her hair. The mother looked at
the child and the child danced and sparkled
and prattled airily along the course of the
streamlet, which kept up a babble, kind, quiet,
soothing, but melancholy. Then the mother
raised her head as though her ears had de-
tected the approach of some one through the
wood. But before I could see who this new-
comer might be, once more the darkness settled down upon the scene.

This time I knew the interval between the
succeeding visions and I waited without impatience; and in due season I found myself gazing at a picture as different as might be from
any I had yet beheld.

In the broad parlor of a house that seemed
to be spacious, a middle - aged lady, of an appearance at once austere and kindly, was looking at a smiling gentleman who was coming
towards her pulling along a little negro girl

about eight or nine years of age.   She was one
of the blackest of her race; and her round,
shining eyes, glittering as glass beads, moved
with quick and restless glances over everything
in the room.   Her woolly hair was braided in
sundry little tails, which stuck out in every
direction.   She was dressed in a single filthy,
ragged garment, made of bagging; and alto-
gether there was something odd and goblin-
like about her appearance.   The severe old
maid examined this strange creature in dismay
and then directed a glance of inquiry at the
gentleman in white.   He smiled again and
gave a signal to the little negro girl.   Whereupon the black eyes glittered with a kind of
wicked drollery, and apparently she began to
sing, keeping time with her hands and feet,
spinning round, clapping her hands, knocking
her knees together, in a wild, fantastic sort of
time; and finally, turning a somersault or two,
she came suddenly down on the carpet, and
stood with her hands folded, and a most sanc-
timonious expression of meekness and solemni-
ty over her face, only broken by the cunning
glances which she shot askance from the corners of her eyes.   The elderly lady stood si-

lent, perfectly paralyzed with amazement, while
the smiling gentleman in white was amused at
her astonishment.

Once more the vision faded. And when,
after the same interval, the darkness began to
disappear again, even while everything was dim
and indistinct I knew that the scene was shifted
from the South to the North. I saw a room
comfortably furnished, with a fire smoulder-
ing in a porcelain stove. In a corner stood a
stripped Christmas-tree, with its candles burned
out. Against the wall between the two doors
was a piano, on which a man was playing—a
man who twisted his head now and again to
look over his shoulder, sometimes at another
and younger man standing by the stove, sometimes at a young woman who was dancing alone
in the centre of the room. This young woman
had draped herself in a long parti-colored
shawl and she held a tambourine in her hand.
There was in her eyes a look of fear, as of one
conscious of an impending misfortune. As I
gazed she danced more and more wildly. The
man standing by the porcelain stove was apparently making suggestions, to which she paid
no heed. At last her hair broke loose and fell

over her shoulders; and even this she did not notice, going on with her dancing as though it were a matter of life and death. Then one of the doors opened and another woman stood on the threshold. The man at the piano ceased playing and left the instrument. The dancer paused unwillingly, and looked pleadingly up into the face of the younger man as he came forward and put his arm around her.

And then once more the light died away and I found myself peering into a void blackness. This time, though I waited long, there were no crackling sparks announcing another inexplicable vision. I peered intently into the stand, but I saw nothing. At last I raised my head and looked about me. Then on the hangings over another of the four stands, over the one opposite to that into which I had been looking, there appeared another message, the letters melting one into another in lines of liquid light; and this told me that in the other stand I could, if I chose, gaze upon combats as memorable as the delectable dances I had been beholding.

I made no hesitation, but crossed the room and took my place before the other stand and began at once to look through the projecting eye-pieces. No sooner had I taken this position than the dots of fire darted across the depth into which I was gazing; and then there came a full clear light as of a cloudless sky, and I saw the walls of an ancient city. At the gates of the city there stood a young man, and toward him there ran a warrior, brandishing a spear, while the bronze of his helmet and his armor gleamed in the sunlight. And trembling seized the young man and he fled in fear; and the warrior darted after him, trusting in his swift feet. Valiant was the flier, but far mightier he who fleetingly pursued him. At last the young man took heart and made a stand against the warrior. They faced each other in fight. The warrior hurled his spear and it went over the young man's head. And the young man then hurled his spear in turn and it struck fair upon the centre of the warrior's shield. Then the young man drew his sharp sword that by his flank hung great and strong. But by some magic the warrior had recovered his spear; and as the young man came forward he hurled it again, and it drove through the neck of the young man at the joint of his armor, and he fell in the dust. After that the sun was darkened; and in a moment more I was looking into an empty blackness.

When again the light returned it was once more with the full blaze of mid-day that the scene was illumined, and the glare of the sun was reflected from the burning sands of the desert. Two or three palms arose near a well, and there two horsemen faced each other warily. One was a Christian knight in a coat of linked mail, over which he wore a surcoat of embroidered cloth, much frayed and bearing more than once the arms of the wearer—a couchant leopard. The other was a Saracen, who was circling swiftly about the knight of the leopard. The crusader suddenly seized the mace which hung at his saddle-bow, and with a strong hand and unerring aim sent it crashing against the head of his foe, who raised his buckler of rhinoceros-hide in time to save his life, though the force of the blow bore him from the saddle. The knight spurred his steed forward, but the Saracen leaped into his seat again without touching the stirrup. While the Christian recovered his mace, the infidel withdrew to a little distance and strung the short bow he carried at his back. Then he circled about his foe, whose armor stood him in good stead, until the seventh shaft apparently found a less perfect part, and the Christian dropped heavily from his horse. But the dismounted Oriental found himself suddenly in the grasp of the European, who had recourse to this artifice to bring his enemy within his reach. The Saracen was saved again by his agility; and loosing his sword-belt, which the knight had grasped, he mounted his watching horse. He had lost his sword and his arrows and his turban, and these disadvantages seemed to incline him for a truce. He approached the Christian with his right hand extended, but no longer in a menacing attitude. What the result of this proffer of a parley might be I could not observe, for the figures became indistinct, as though a cloud had settled down on them; and in a few seconds more all was blank before me.

When the next scene grew slowly into view I thought for a moment it might be a continuation of the preceding, for the country I beheld was also soaking in the hot sunlight of the South, and there was also a mounted knight in armor. A second glance undeceived me.

This knight was old and thin and worn, and his armor was broken and pieced, and his helmet was but a barber's basin, and his steed was a pitiful skeleton. His countenance was sorrowful indeed, but there was that in his manner which would stop any man from denying his nobility. His eye was fired with a high purpose and a lofty resolve. In the distance before him were a group of windmills waving their arms in the air, and the knight urged forward his wretched horse as though to charge them. Upon an ass behind him was a fellow of the baser sort, a genial, simple follower, seemingly serving him as his squire. As the knight pricked forward his sorry steed and couched his lance, the attendant apparently appealed to him, and tried to explain, and even ventured on expostulation. But the knight gave no heed to the protests of the squire, who shook his head and dutifully followed his master. What the issue of this unequal combat was to be I could not see, for the inexorable veil of darkness fell swiftly.

Even after the stray sparks had again flitted through the blackness into which I was gazing daylight did not return, and it was with diffi-

culty I was able at last to make out a vague
street in a mediæval city doubtfully outlined
by the hidden moon. From a window high
above the stones there came a faint glimmer.
Under this window stood a soldier worn with
the wars, who carried himself as though glad
now to be at home again. He seemed to hear
approaching feet, and he withdrew into the
shadow as two others advanced. One of these
was a handsome youth with an eager face, in
which spirituality and sensuality contended.
The other was older, of an uncertain age, and
his expression was mocking and evil; he carried some sort of musical instrument, and to
this he seemed to sing while the younger man
looked up at the window. The soldier came
forward angrily and dashed the instrument to
the ground with his sword. Then the new-
comers drew also, and the elder guarded while
the younger thrust. There were a few swift
passes, and then the younger of the two lunged
fiercely, and the soldier fell back on the stones
wounded to the death. Without a glance behind them, the two who had withstood his on-
slaught withdrew, as the window above opened
and a fair-haired girl leaned forth.

Then nothing was visible, until after an interval the light once more returned and I saw a sadder scene than any yet. In a hollow of the bare mountains a little knot of men in dark-blue uniforms were centred about their commander, whose long locks floated from beneath his broad hat. Around this small band of no more than a score of soldiers, thousands of red Indians were raging, with exultant hate in their eyes. The bodies of dead comrades lay in narrowing circles about the thinning group of blue-coats. The red men were picking off their few surviving foes, one by one; and the white men could do nothing, for their cartridges were all gone. They stood at bay, valiant and defiant, despite their many wounds; but the line of their implacable foemen was drawn tighter and tighter about them, and one after another they fell forward dying or dead, until at last only the long-haired commander was left, sore wounded but unconquered in spirit.

When this picture of strong men facing death fearlessly was at last dissolved into darkness like the others that had gone before, I had an inward monition that it was the last that would be shown me; and so it was, for although I kept my place at the stand for two or three minutes more, no warning sparks dispersed the opaque depth.

When I raised my head from the eye-pieces, I became conscious that I was not alone. Almost in the centre of the circular hall stood a middle-aged man of distinguished appearance, whose eyes were fixed upon me. I wondered who he was, and whence he had come, and how he had entered, and what it might be that he wished with me. I caught a glimpse of a smile that lurked vaguely on his lips. Neither this smile nor the expression of his eyes was forbidding, though both were uncanny and inexplicable. He seemed to be conscious of a remoteness which would render futile any effort of his towards friendliness.

How long we stood thus staring the one at the other I do not know. My heart beat heavily and my tongue refused to move when at last I tried to break the silence.

Then he spoke, and his voice was low and strong and sweet.

"You are welcome," he began, and I noted that the accent was slightly foreign, Italian perhaps, or it might be French. "I am glad always to show the visions I have under my control to those who will appreciate them."

I tried to stammer forth a few words of thanks and of praise for what I had seen.

"Did you recognize the strange scenes shown to you by these two instruments?" he asked, after bowing gently in acknowledgment of my awkward compliments.

Then I plucked up courage and made bold to express to him the surprise I had felt, not only at the marvellous vividness with which the actions had been repeated before my eyes, like life itself in form and in color and in motion, but also at the startling fact that some of the things I had been shown were true and some were false. Some of them had happened actually to real men and women of flesh and blood, while others were but bits of vain imagining of those who tell tales as an art and as a means of livelihood.

I expressed myself as best I could, clumsily, no doubt; but he listened patiently and with the smile of toleration on his lips.

"Yes," he answered, "I understand your surprise that the facts and the fictions are mingled together in these visions of mine as though there was little to choose between them. You are not the first to wonder or to express that wonder; and the rest of them were young like you. When you are as old as I am—when you have lived as long as I—when you have seen as much of life as I—then you will know, as I know, that fact is often inferior to fiction, and that it is often also one and the same thing; for what might have been is often quite as true as what actually was?"

I did not know what to say in answer to this, and so I said nothing.

"What would you say to me," he went on—and now it seemed to me that his smile suggested rather pitying condescension than kindly toleration—"what would you say to me, if I were to tell you that I myself have seen all the many visions unrolled before you in these instruments? What would you say, if I declared that I had gazed on the dances of Salome and of Esmeralda? that I had beheld the combat of Achilles and Hector and the mounted fight of Saladin and the Knight of the Leopard?"

"You are not Time himself?" I asked in amaze.

He laughed lightly, and without bitterness or mockery.

"No," he answered, promptly, "I am not Time himself. And why should you think so? Have I a scythe? Have I an hour-glass? Have I a forelock? Do I look so very old, then?"

I examined him more carefully to answer this last question, and the more I scrutinized him the more difficult I found it to declare his age. At first I had thought him to be forty, perhaps, or of a certainty less than fifty. But now, though his hair was black, though his eye was bright, though his step was firm, though his gestures were free and sweeping, I had my doubts; and I thought I could perceive, one after another, many impalpable signs of extreme old age.

Then, all at once, he grew restive under my fixed gaze.

"But it is not about me that we need to waste time now," he said, impatiently. "You have seen what two of my instruments contain; would you like now to examine the contents of the other two?"

I answered in the affirmative.

" The two you have looked into are gratui-
tous," he continued. "For what you beheld
in them there is no charge. But a sight of the
visions in the other two or in either one of
them must be paid for. So far, you are welcome as my guest; but if you wish to see any
more you must pay the price."

I asked what the charge was, as I thrust my
hand into my pocket to be certain that I had
my purse with me.

He saw my gesture, and he smiled once
more.

" The visions I can set before you in those
two instruments you have not yet looked
into are visions of your own life," he said.
" In that stand there," and he indicated one
behind my back, " you can see five of the
most important episodes of your past."

I withdrew my hand from my pocket. " I
thank you," I said, " but I know my own past,
and I have no wish to see it again, however
cheap the spectacle."

" Then you will be more interested in the
fourth of my instruments," he said, as he
waved his thin, delicate hand towards the

4

stand which stood in front of me. "In this you can see your future!"

I made an involuntary step forward; and then, at a second thought, I shrank back again.

"The price of this is not high," he continued, "and it is not payable in money."

"How, then, should I buy it?" I asked, doubtingly.

"In life!" he answered, gravely. "The vision of life must be paid for in life itself. For every ten years of the future which I may unroll before you here, you must assign me a year of life — twelve months — to do with as I will."

Strange as it seems to me now, I did not doubt that he could do as he declared. I hesitated, and then I fixed my resolve.

"Thank you," I said, and I saw that he was awaiting my decision eagerly. "Thank you again for what I have already seen and for what you proffer me. But my past I have lived once, and there is no need to turn over again the leaves of that dead record. And the future I must face as best I may, the more bravely, I think, that I do not know what it holds in store for me."

"The price is low," he urged.

"It must be lower still," I answered; "it might be nothing at all, and I should still decline. I cannot afford to be impatient now and to borrow knowledge of the future. I shall know all in good time."

He seemed not a little disappointed as I said this.

Then he made a final appeal: "Would you not wish to know even the matter of your end?"

"No," I answered. "That is no temptation to me, for whatever it may be I must find fortitude to undergo it somehow, whether I am to pass away in my sleep in my bed, or whether I shall have to withstand the chances of battle and murder and sudden death."

"That is your last word?" he inquired.

"I thank you again for what I have seen," I responded, bowing again; "but my decision is final."

"Then I will detain you no longer," he said, haughtily, and he walked towards the circling curtains and swept two of them aside. They draped themselves back, and I saw before me

an opening like that through which I had
entered.

I followed him, and the curtains dropped behind me as I passed into the insufficiently illuminated passage beyond. I thought that the
mysterious being with whom I had been con-
versing had preceded me, but before I had gone
twenty paces I found that I was alone. I
pushed ahead, and my path twisted and turned
on itself and rose and fell irregularly like that
by means of which I had made my way into
the unknown edifice. At last I picked my
steps down winding stairs, and at the foot I
saw the outline of a door. I pushed it back,
and I found myself in the open air.

I was in a broad street, and over my head an
electric light suddenly flared out and white-
washed the pavement at my feet. At the
corner a train of the elevated railroad rushed
by with a clattering roar and a trailing plume
of white steam. Then a cable-car clanged
past with incessant bangs upon its gong. Thus
it was that I came back to the world of
actuality.

I turned to get my bearings, that I might
find my way home again. I was standing

almost in front of a shop, the windows of which were filled with framed engravings.

One of these caught my eye, and I confess that I was surprised. It was a portrait of a man—it was a portrait of the man with whom I had been talking.

I went close to the window, that I might see it better. The electric light emphasized the lines of the high-bred face, with its sombre searching eyes and the air of old-world breeding. There could be no doubt whatever that the original of this portrait was the man from whom I had just parted. By the costume I knew that the original had lived in the last century; and the legend beneath the head, engraved in a flowing script, asserted this to be a likeness of "*Monsieur le Comte de Cagli-ostro.*"

(1895.)

THE DREAM-GOWN OF THE JAPANESE
AMBASSADOR

THE DREAM-GOWN OF THE
JAPANESE AMBASSADOR

I

FTER arranging the Egyptian and Mexican pottery so as to contrast agreeably with the Dutch and the German beer-mugs on the top of the bookcase that ran along one wall of the sitting-room, Cosmo Waynflete went back into the bedroom and took from a half-empty trunk the little cardboard boxes in which he kept the collection of playing-cards, and of all manner of outlandish equivalents for these simple instruments of fortune, picked up here and there during his two or three years of dilettante travelling in strange countries. At the same time he brought out a Japanese crystal ball, which he stood upon its silver tripod, placing it on a little table in one of the windows on each side of the fireplace; and there the rays of the westering sun lighted it up at once into translucent loveliness.

The returned wanderer looked out of the window and saw on one side the graceful and vigorous tower of the Madison Square Garden, with its Diana turning in the December wind, while in the other direction he could look down on the frozen paths of Union Square, only a block distant, but as far below him almost as though he were gazing down from a balloon. Then he stepped back into the sitting-room itself, and noted the comfortable furniture and wood-fire crackling in friendly fashion on the hearth, and his own personal belongings, scattered here and there as though they were settling themselves for a stay. Having arrived from Europe only that morning, he could not but hold himself lucky to have found these rooms taken for him by the old friend to whom he had announced his return, and with whom he was to eat his Christmas dinner that evening. He had not been on shore more than six or seven hours, and yet the most of his odds and ends were unpacked and already in place as though they

belonged in this new abode.   It was true that
he had toiled unceasingly to accomplish this,
and as he stood there in his shirt-sleeves,
admiring the results of his labors, he was conscious also that his muscles were fatigued, and
that the easy-chair before the fire opened its
arms temptingly.

He went again into the bedroom, and took
from one of his many trunks a long, loose garment of pale-gray silk.   Apparently this beautiful robe was intended to serve as a dressing-
gown, and as such Cosmo Waynflete utilized it
immediately.   The ample folds fell softly about
him, and the rich silk itself seemed to be soothing to his limbs, so delicate was its fibre and
so carefully had it been woven.   Around the
full skirt there was embroidery of threads of
gold, and again on the open and flowing sleeves.
With the skilful freedom of Japanese art the
pattern of this decoration seemed to suggest
the shrubbery about a spring, for there were
strange plants with huge leaves broadly outlined by the golden threads, and in the midst
of them water was seen bubbling from the
earth and lapping gently over the edge of the
fountain.   As the returned wanderer thrust

his arms into the dressing-gown with its symbolic embroidery on the skirt and sleeves, he remembered distinctly the dismal day when he had bought it in a little curiosity-shop in Nuremberg; and as he fastened across his chest one by one the loops of silken cord to the three coins which served as buttons down the front of the robe, he recalled also the time and the place where he had picked up each of these pieces of gold and silver, one after another. The first of them was a Persian daric, which he had purchased from a dealer on the Grand Canal in Venice; and the second was a Spanish peso struck under Philip II. at Potosi, which he had found in a stall on the embankment of the Quay Voltaire, in Paris; and the third was a York shilling, which he had bought from the man who had turned it up in ploughing a field that sloped to the Hudson near Sleepy Hollow.

Having thus wrapped himself in this unusual dressing-gown with its unexpected buttons of gold and silver, Cosmo Waynflete went back into the front room. He dropped into the arm-chair before the fire. It was with a smile of physical satisfaction that he stretched out his feet to the hickory blaze.

The afternoon was drawing on, and in New York the sun sets early on Christmas day. The red rays shot into the window almost horizontally, and they filled the crystal globe with a curious light.   Cosmo Waynflete lay back in his easy-chair, with his Japanese robe about him, and gazed intently at the beautiful ball which seemed like a bubble of air and water.   His mind went back to the afternoon in April, two years before, when he had found that crystal sphere in a Japanese shop within sight of the incomparable Fugiyama.

II

As he peered into its transparent depths, with his vision focused upon the spot of light where the rays of the setting sun touched it into flame, he was but little surprised to discover that he could make out tiny figures in the crystal. For the moment this strange thing seemed to him perfectly natural. And the movements of these little men and women interested him so much that he watched them as they went to and fro, sweeping a roadway with large brooms. Thus it happened that the fixity of his gaze was intensified. And so it was that in a few minutes he saw with no astonishment that he was one of the group himself, he himself in the rich and stately attire of a samurai. From the instant that Cosmo Waynflete discovered himself among the people whom he saw moving before him, as his eyes were fastened on the illuminated dot in the transparent ball, he ceased to see them as little figures, and he accepted them as of the full stature of man. This increase in their size was no more a source of wonderment to him than it had been to discern himself in the midst of them. He accepted both of these marvellous things without question — indeed, with no thought at all that they were in any way peculiar or abnormal. Not only this, but thereafter he seemed to have transferred his personality to the Cosmo Waynflete who was a Japanese samurai and to have abandoned entirely the Cosmo Waynflete who was an American traveller, and who had just returned to New York that Christmas morning. So completely did the Japanese identity dominate that the existence of the American identity was wholly unknown to him. It was as though the American had gone to sleep in New York at the end of the nineteenth century, and had waked a Japanese in Nippon in the beginning of the eighteenth century.

With his sword by his side—a Murimasa blade, likely to bring bad luck to the wearer sooner or later—he had walked from his own house in the quarter of Kioto which is called Yamashina to the quarter which is called

Yoshiwara, a place of ill repute, where dwell women of evil life, and where roysterers and drunkards come by night. He knew that the sacred duty of avenging his master's death had led him to cast off his faithful wife so that he might pretend to riot in debauchery at the Three Sea-Shores. The fame of his shameful doings had spread abroad, and it must soon come to the ears of the man whom he wished to take unawares. Now he was lying prone in the street, seemingly sunk in a drunken slumber, so that men might see him and carry the news to the treacherous assassin of his beloved master. As he lay there that afternoon, he revolved in his mind the devices he should use to make away with his enemy when the hour might be ripe at last for the accomplishment of his holy revenge. To himself he called the roll of his fellow-ronins, now biding their time, as he was, and ready always to obey his orders and to follow his lead to the death, when at last the sun should rise on the day of vengeance.

So he gave no heed to the scoffs and the jeers of those who passed along the street, laughing him to scorn as they beheld him lying there in a stupor from excessive drink at that inordinate hour of the day. And among those who came by at last was a man from Satsuma, who was moved to voice the reproaches of all that saw this sorry sight.

"Is not this Oishi Kuranosuke," said the man from Satsuma, " who was a councillor of Asano Takumi no Kami, and who, not having the heart to avenge his lord, gives himself up to women and wine? See how he lies drunk in the public street! Faithless beast! Fool and craven! Unworthy of the name of a samurai!"

And with that the man from Satsuma trod on him as he lay there, and spat upon him, and went away indignantly. The spies of Kotsuke no Suke heard what the man from Satsuma had said, and they saw how he had spurned the prostrate samurai with his foot ; and they went their way to report to their master that he need no longer have any fear of the councillors of Asano Takumi no Kami. All this the man, lying prone in the dust of the street, noted ; and it made his heart glad, for then he made sure that the day was soon coming when he could do his duty at last and take vengeance for the death of his master.

III

He lay there longer than he knew, and the twilight settled down at last, and the evening stars came out. And then, after a while, and by imperceptible degrees, Cosmo Waynflete became conscious that the scene had changed and that he had changed with it. He was no longer in Japan, but in Persia. He was no longer lying like a drunkard in the street of a city, but slumbering like a weary soldier in a little oasis by the side of a spring in the midst of a sandy desert. He was asleep, and his faithful horse was unbridled that it might crop the grass at will.

The air was hot and thick, and the leaves of the slim tree above him were never stirred by a wandering wind. Yet now and again there came from the darkness a faintly fetid odor. The evening wore on and still he slept, until at length in the silence of the night a strange huge creature wormed its way steadily

out of its lair amid the trees, and drew near
the sleeping man to devour him fiercely.   But
the horse neighed vehemently and beat the
ground with his hoofs and waked his master.
Then the hideous monster vanished; and the
man, aroused from his sleep, saw nothing, although the evil smell still lingered in the
sultry atmosphere.   He lay down again once
more, thinking that for once his steed had
given a false alarm.   Again the grisly dragon
drew nigh, and again the courser notified its
rider, and again the man could make out
nothing in the darkness of the night; and
again he was wellnigh stifled by the foul
emanation that trailed in the wake of the
misbegotten creature.   He rebuked his horse
and laid him down once more.

A third time the dreadful beast approached,
and a third time the faithful charger awoke
its angry master.   But there came the breath
of a gentle breeze, so that the man did not
fear to fill his lungs; and there was a vague
light in the heavens now, so that he could
dimly discern his mighty enemy; and at once
he girded himself for the fight.   The scaly
monster came full at him with dripping fangs,

its mighty body thrusting forward its huge and hideous head. The man met the attack without fear and smote the beast full on the crest, but the blow rebounded from its coat of mail.

Then the faithful horse sprang forward and bit the dreadful creature full upon the neck and tore away the scales, so that its master's sword could pierce the armored hide. So the man was able to dissever the ghastly head and thus to slay the monstrous dragon. The blackness of night wrapped him about once more as he fell on his knees and gave thanks for his victory; and the wind died away again.

IV

ONLY a few minutes later, so it seemed to
him, Cosmo Waynflete became doubtfully
aware of another change of time and place—
of another transformation of his own being.
He knew himself to be alone once more, and
even without his trusty charger. Again he
found himself groping in the dark. But in a
little while there was a faint radiance of light,
and at last the moon came out behind a tower.
Then he saw that he was not by the roadside
in Japan or in the desert of Persia, but now
in some unknown city of Southern Europe,
where the architecture was hispano-moresque.
By the silver rays of the moon he was able to
make out the beautiful design damascened
upon the blade of the sword which he held
now in his hand ready drawn for self-defence.

Then he heard hurried footfalls down the
empty street, and a man rushed around the
corner pursued by two others, who had also

weapons in their hands. For a moment Cosmo Waynflete was a Spaniard, and to him it was a point of honor to aid the weaker party. He cried to the fugitive to pluck up heart and to withstand the enemy stoutly. But the hunted man fled on, and after him went one of the pursuers, a tall, thin fellow, with a long black cloak streaming behind him as he ran.

The other of the two, a handsome lad with fair hair, came to a halt and crossed swords with Cosmo, and soon showed himself to be skilled in the art of fence. So violent was the young fellow's attack that in the ardor of self-defence Cosmo ran the boy through the body before he had time to hold his hand or even to reflect.

The lad toppled over sideways. "Oh, my mother!" he cried, and in a second he was dead. While Cosmo bent over the body, hasty footsteps again echoed along the silent thoroughfare. Cosmo peered around the corner, and by the struggling moonbeams he could see that it was the tall, thin fellow in the black cloak, who was returning with half a score of retainers, all armed, and some of them bearing torches.

Cosmo turned and fled swiftly, but being a stranger in the city he soon lost himself in its tortuous streets. Seeing a light in a window and observing a vine that trailed from the balcony before it, he climbed up boldly, and found himself face to face with a gray-haired lady, whose visage was beautiful and kindly and noble. In a few words he told her his plight and besought sanctuary. She listened to him in silence, with exceeding courtesy of manner, as though she were weighing his words before making up her mind. She raised the lamp on her table and let its beams fall on his lineaments. And still she made no answer to his appeal.

Then came a glare of torches in the street below and a knocking at the door. Then at last the old lady came to a resolution; she lifted the tapestry at the head of her bed and told him to bestow himself there. No sooner was he hidden than the tall, thin man in the long black cloak entered hastily. He greeted the elderly lady as his aunt, and he told her that her son had been set upon by a stranger in the street and had been slain. She gave a great cry and never took her eyes from his face. Then he said that a servant had seen an unknown man climb to the balcony of her house. What if it were the assassin of her son? The blood left her face and she clutched at the table behind her, as she gave orders to have the house searched.

When the room was empty at last she went to the head of the bed and bade the man concealed there to come forth and begone, but to cover his face, that she might not be forced to know him again. So saying, she dropped on her knees before a crucifix, while he slipped out of the window again and down to the deserted street.

He sped to the corner and turned it undiscovered, and breathed a sigh of relief and of regret. He kept on steadily, gliding stealthily along in the shadows, until he found himself at the city gate as the bell of the cathedral tolled the hour of midnight.

How it was that he passed through the gate he could not declare with precision, for seemingly a mist had settled about him. Yet a few minutes later he saw that in some fashion he must have got beyond the walls of the town, for he recognized the open country all around. And, oddly enough, he now discovered himself to be astride a bony steed. He could not say what manner of horse it was he was riding, but he felt sure that it was not the faithful charger that had saved his life in Persia, once upon a time, in days long gone by, as it seemed to him then. He was not in Persia now—of that he was certain, nor in Japan, nor in the Iberian peninsula. Where he was he did not know.

In the dead hush of midnight he could hear the barking of a dog on the opposite shore of a dusky and indistinct waste of waters that spread itself far below him. The night grew darker and darker, the stars seemed to sink deeper in the sky, and driving clouds occasionally hid them from his sight. He had never felt so lonely and dismal. In the centre of the road stood an enormous tulip-tree; its limbs were gnarled and fantastic, large enough to form trunks for ordinary trees, twisting down almost to the earth, and rising again into the air. As he approached this fearful tree he thought he saw something white hanging in the midst of it, but on looking more narrowly he perceived it was a place where it had been scathed by lightning and the white wood laid bare. About two hundred yards from the tree a small brook crossed the road; and as he drew near he beheld—on the margin of this brook, and in the dark shadow of the grove—he beheld something huge, misshapen, black, and towering. It stirred not, but seemed gathered up in the gloom like some gigantic monster ready to spring upon the traveller.

He demanded, in stammering accents, "Who are you?" He received no reply. He repeated his demand in a still more agitated voice. Still there was no answer. And then the shadowy object of alarm put itself in motion, and with a scramble and a bound stood in the middle of the road. He appeared to be a horseman of large dimensions and mounted on a black horse of powerful frame. Having no relish for this strange midnight companion, Cosmo Waynflete urged on his steed in hopes of leaving the apparition behind; but the stranger quickened his horse also to an equal pace. And when the first horseman pulled up, thinking to lag behind, the second did likewise. There was something in the moody and dogged silence of this pertinacious companion that was mysterious and appalling. It was soon fearfully accounted for. On mounting a rising ground which brought the figure of his fellow-traveller against the sky, gigantic in height and muffled in a cloak, he was horror-struck to discover the stranger was headless! —but his horror was still more increased in observing that the head which should have rested on the shoulders was carried before the body on the pommel of the saddle.

The terror of Cosmo Waynflete rose to desperation, and he spurred his steed suddenly in the hope of giving his weird companion the slip. But the headless horseman started full

jump with him. His own horse, as though possessed by a demon, plunged headlong down the
hill.   He could hear, however, the black steed
panting and blowing close behind him; he
even fancied that he felt the hot breath of the
pursuer.   When he ventured at last to cast a
look behind, he saw the goblin rising in the
stirrups, and in the very act of hurling at him
the grisly head.   He fell out of the saddle to
the ground; and the black steed and the goblin rider passed by him like a whirlwind.

VI

How long he lay there by the roadside, stunned and motionless, he could not guess; but when he came to himself at last the sun was already high in the heavens. He discovered himself to be reclining on the tall grass of a pleasant graveyard which surrounded a tiny country church in the outskirts of a pretty little village. It was in the early summer, and the foliage was green above him as the boughs swayed gently to and fro in the morning breeze. The birds were singing gayly as they flitted about over his head. The bees hummed along from flower to flower. At last, so it seemed to him, he had come into a land of peace and quiet, where there was rest and comfort and where no man need go in fear of his life. It was a country where vengeance was not a duty and where midnight combats were not a custom. He found himself smiling as he thought that a grisly dragon and a goblin rider would be equally out of place in this laughing landscape.

Then the bell in the steeple of the little church began to ring merrily, and he rose to his feet in expectation. All of a sudden the knowledge came to him why it was that they were ringing. He wondered then why the coming of the bride was thus delayed. He knew himself to be a lover, with life opening brightly before him ; and the world seemed to him sweeter than ever before and more beautiful.

Then at last the girl whom he loved with his whole heart and who had promised to marry him appeared in the distance, and he thought he had never seen her look more lovely. As he beheld his bridal party approaching, he slipped into the church to await her at the altar. The sunshine fell full upon the portal and made a halo about the girl's head as she crossed the threshold.

But even when the bride stood by his side and the clergyman had begun the solemn service of the church the bells kept on, and soon their chiming became a clangor, louder and sharper and more insistent.

VII

So clamorous and so persistent was the ringing that Cosmo Waynflete was roused at last. He found himself suddenly standing on his feet, with his hand clutching the back of the chair in which he had been sitting before the fire when the rays of the setting sun had set long ago. The room was dark, for it was lighted now only by the embers of the burntout fire; and the electric bell was ringing steadily, as though the man outside the door had resolved to waken the seven sleepers.

Then Cosmo Waynflete was wide-awake again; and he knew where he was once more — not in Japan, not in Persia, not in Lisbon, not in Sleepy Hollow, but here in New York, in his own room, before his own fire. He opened the door at once and admitted his friend, Paul Stuyvesant.

"It isn't dinner-time, is it?" he asked. "I'm not late, am I? The fact is, I've been asleep."

"It is so good of you to confess that," his friend answered, laughing; "although the length of time you kept me waiting and ringing might have led me to suspect it. No, you are not late and it is not dinner-time. I've come around to have another little chat with you before dinner, that's all."

"Take this chair, old man," said Cosmo, as he threw another hickory-stick on the fire. Then he lighted the gas and sat down by the side of his friend.

"This chair is comfortable, for a fact," Stuyvesant declared, stretching himself out luxuriously. "No wonder you went to sleep. What did you dream of?—strange places you had seen in your travels or the homely scenes of your native land."

Waynflete looked at his friend for a moment without answering the question. He was startled as he recalled the extraordinary series of adventures which had fallen to his lot since he had fixed his gaze on the crystal ball. It seemed to him as though he had been whirled through space and through time.

"I suppose every man is always the hero of his own dreams," he began, doubtfully.

"Of course," his friend returned; "in sleep our natural and healthy egotism is absolutely unrestrained. It doesn't make any matter where the scene is laid or whether the play is a comedy or a tragedy, the dreamer has always the centre of the stage, with the calcium light turned full on him."

"That's just it," Waynflete went on; "this dream of mine makes me feel as if I were an actor, and as if I had been playing many parts, one after the other, in the swiftest succession. They are not familiar to me, and yet I confess to a vague feeling of unoriginality. It is as though I were a plagiarist of adventure—if that be a possible supposition. I have just gone through these startling situations myself, and yet I'm sure that they have all of them happened before — although, perhaps, not to any one man. Indeed, no one man could have had all these adventures of mine, because I see now that I have been whisked through the centuries and across the hemispheres with a suddenness possible only in dreams. Yet all my experiences seem somehow second-hand, and not really my own."

"Picked up here and there—like your bricà-brac?" suggested Stuyvesant. "But what are these alluring adventures of yours that stretched through the ages and across the continents?"

Then, knowing how fond his friend was of solving mysteries and how proud he was of his skill in this art, Cosmo Waynflete narrated his dream as it has been set down in these pages.

When he had made an end, Paul Stuyvesant's first remark was: "I'm sorry I happened along just then and waked you up before you had time to get married."

His second remark followed half a minute later.

"I see how it was," he said; "you were sitting in this chair and looking at that crystal ball, which focussed the level rays of the setting sun, I suppose? Then it is plain enough —you hypnotized yourself!"

"I have heard that such a thing is possible," responded Cosmo.

"Possible?" Stuyvesant returned, "it is certain! But what is more curious is the new way in which you combined your self-hypnotism with crystal-gazing. You have heard of scrying, I suppose?"

"You mean the practice of looking into a drop of water or a crystal ball or anything of that sort," said Cosmo, "and of seeing things in it—of seeing people moving about?"

"That's just what I do mean," his friend returned. "And that's just what you have been doing. You fixed your gaze on the ball, and so hypnotized yourself; and then, in the intensity of your vision, you were able to see figures in the crystal—with one of which visualized emanations you immediately identified yourself. That's easy enough, I think. But I don't see what suggested to you your separate experiences. I recognize them, of course—"

"You recognize them?" cried Waynflete, in wonder.

"I can tell you where you borrowed every one of your adventures," Stuyvesant replied, "But what I'd like to know now is what suggested to you just those particular characters and situations, and not any of the many others also stored away in your subconsciousness."

So saying, he began to look about the room.

"My subconsciousness?" repeated Waynflete. "Have I ever been a samurai in my subconsciousness?"

Paul Stuyvesant looked at Cosmo Wayn-flete for nearly a minute without reply. Then all the answer he made was to say : " That's a queer dressing-gown you have on."

" It is time I took it off," said the other, as he twisted himself out of its clinging folds. "It is a beautiful specimen of weaving, isn't it ? I call it the dream-gown of the Japanese ambassador, for although I bought it in a curiosity-shop in Nuremberg, it was once, I really believe, the slumber-robe of an Oriental envoy."

Stuyvesant took the silken garment from his friend's hand.

" Why did the Japanese ambassador sell you his dream-gown in a Nuremberg curiosity-shop ?" he asked.

" He didn't," Waynflete explained. " I never saw the ambassador, and neither did the old German lady who kept the shop. She told me she bought it from a Japanese acrobat who was out of an engagement and desperately hard up. But she told me also that the acrobat had told her that the garment had belonged to an ambassador who had given it to him as a reward of his skill, and that he never would have

parted with it if he had not been dead-
broke."

Stuyvesant held the robe up to the light
and inspected the embroidery on the skirt of it.

" Yes," he said, at last, "this would account
for it, I suppose. This bit here was probably
meant to suggest ' the well where the head
was washed,'—see ?"

" I see that those lines may be meant to
represent the outline of a spring of water,
but I don't see what that has to do with my
dream," Waynflete answered.

" Don't you ?" Stuyvesant returned. "Then
I'll show you. You had on this silk garment
embroidered here with an outline of the well
in which was washed the head of Kotsuke no
Suke, the man whom the Forty-Seven Ronins
killed. You know the story ?"

" I read it in Japan, but—" began Cosmo.

" You had that story stored away in your
subconsciousness," interrupted his friend.
" And when you hypnotized yourself by peering into the crystal ball, this embroidery it
was which suggested to you to see yourself as
the hero of the tale—Oishi Kuranosuke, the
chief of the Forty-Seven Ronins, the faithful

follower who avenged his master by pretending to be vicious and dissipated — just like Brutus and Lorenzaccio—until the enemy was off his guard and open to attack."

"I think I do recall the tale of the Forty-Seven Ronins, but only very vaguely," said the hero of the dream. "For all I know I may have had the adventure of Oishi Kuranosuke laid on the shelf somewhere in my sub-consciousness, as you want me to believe. But how about my Persian dragon and my Iberian noblewoman?"

Paul Stuyvesant was examining the dream-gown of the Japanese ambassador with minute care. Suddenly he said, "Oh!" and then he looked up at Cosmo Waynflete and asked: "What are those buttons? They seem to be old coins."

"They are old coins," the other answered; "it was a fancy of mine to utilize them on that Japanese dressing-gown. They are all different, you see. The first is—"

"Persian, isn't it?" interrupted Stuyvesant.

"Yes," Waynflete explained, "it is a Persian daric. And the second is a Spanish peso made at Potosi under Philip II. for use in America.

And the third is a York shilling, one of the
coins in circulation here in New York at the
time of the Revolution—I got that one, in fact,
from the farmer who ploughed it up in a field
at Tarrytown, near Sunnyside."

"Then there are three of your adventures
accounted for, Cosmo, and easily enough,"
Paul commented, with obvious satisfaction at
his own explanation. "Just as the embroidery
on the silk here suggested to you—after you
had hypnotized yourself—that you were the
chief of the Forty-Seven Ronins, so this first
coin here in turn suggested to you that you
were Rustem, the hero of the ' Epic of Kings.'
You have read the ' Shah-Nameh ? ' "

"I remember Firdausi's poem after a fashion only," Cosmo answered. "Was not Rustem a Persian Hercules, so to speak ? "

" That's it precisely," the other responded,
"and he had seven labors to perform; and
you dreamed the third of them, the slaying of
the grisly dragon. For my own part, I think I
should have preferred the fourth of them, the
meeting with the lovely enchantress; but that's
neither here nor there."

"It seems to me I do recollect something

about that fight of Rustem and the strange
beast. The faithful horse's name was Rakush,
wasn't it?" asked Waynflete.

"If you can recollect the 'Shah-Nameh,'"
Stuyvesant pursued, "no doubt you can recall
also Beaumont and Fletcher's 'Custom of the
Country?' That's where you got the midnight duel in Lisbon and the magnanimous
mother, you know."

"No, I didn't know," the other declared.

"Well, you did, for all that," Paul went on.
"The situation is taken from one in a drama
of Calderon's, and it was much strengthened
in the taking. You may not now remember
having read the play, but the incident must
have been familiar to you, or else your subconsciousness couldn't have yielded it up to you
so readily at the suggestion of the Spanish
coin, could it?"

"I did read a lot of Elizabethan drama
in my senior year at college," admitted Cosmo, "and this piece of Beaumont and Fletcher's may have been one of those I read; but I
totally fail to recall now what it was all
about."

"You won't have the cheek to declare that

you don't remember the 'Legend of Sleepy Hollow,' will you?" asked Stuyvesant. "Very obviously it was the adventure of Ichabod Crane and the Headless Horseman that the York shilling suggested to you."

"I'll admit that I do recollect Irving's story now," the other confessed.

So the embroidery on the dream-gown gives the first of your strange situations; and the three others were suggested by the coins you have been using as buttons," said Paul Stuyvesant. "There is only one thing now that puzzles me: that is the country church and the noon wedding and the beautiful bride."

And with that he turned over the folds of the silken garment that hung over his arm.

Cosmo Waynflete hesitated a moment and a blush mantled his cheek. Then he looked his friend in the face and said: "I think I can account for my dreaming about her—I can account for that easily enough."

"So can I," said Paul Stuyvesant, as he held up the photograph of a lovely American girl that he had just found in the pocket of the dream-gown of the Japanese ambassador.

(1896.)

THE RIVAL GHOSTS

THE RIVAL GHOSTS

THE good ship sped on her way across the calm Atlantic. It was an outward passage, according to the little charts which the company had charily distributed, but most of the passengers were homeward bound, after a summer of rest and recreation, and they were counting the days before they might hope to see Fire Island Light. On the lee side of the boat, comfortably sheltered from the wind, and just by the door of the captain's room (which was theirs during the day), sat a little group of returning Americans. The Duchess (she was down on the purser's list as Mrs. Martin, but her friends and familiars called her the Duchess of Washington Square) and Baby Van Rensselaer (she was quite old enough to vote, had her sex been entitled to that duty, but as the younger of two sisters she was still the baby of the family)—the Duchess and Baby Van Rensselaer were discussing the pleasant English voice and the not unpleasant English accent of a manly young lordling who was going to America for sport. Uncle Larry and Dear Jones were enticing each other into a bet on the ship's run of the morrow.

"I'll give you two to one she don't make 420," said Dear Jones.

"I'll take it," answered Uncle Larry. "We made 427 the fifth day last year." It was Uncle Larry's seventeenth visit to Europe, and this was therefore his thirty-fourth voyage.

"And when did you get in?" asked Baby Van Rensselaer. "I don't care a bit about the run, so long as we get in soon."

"We crossed the bar Sunday night, just seven days after we left Queenstown, and we dropped anchor off Quarantine at three o'clock on Monday morning."

"I hope we sha'n't do that this time. I can't seem to sleep any when the boat stops."

"I can, but I didn't," continued Uncle Larry, "because my state-room was the most for'ard in the boat, and the donkey-engine that let down the anchor was right over my head."

"So you got up and saw the sun rise over the bay," said Dear Jones, "with the electric lights of the city twinkling in the distance, and the first faint flush of the dawn in the east just over Fort Lafayette, and the rosy tinge which spread softly upward, and—"

"Did you both come back together?" asked the Duchess.

"Because he has crossed thirty-four times you must not suppose he has a monopoly in sunrises," retorted Dear Jones. "No; this was my own sunrise; and a mighty pretty one it was too."

"I'm not matching sunrises with you," remarked Uncle Larry calmly; "but I'm willing to back a merry jest called forth by my sunrise against any two merry jests called forth by yours."

"I confess reluctantly that my sunrise evoked no merry jest at all." Dear Jones was an honest man, and would scorn to invent a merry jest on the spur of the moment.

" That's where my sunrise has the call," said Uncle Larry, complacently.

" What was the merry jest?" was Baby Van Rensselaer's inquiry, the natural result of a feminine curiosity thus artistically excited.

" Well, here it is. I was standing aft, near a patriotic American and a wandering Irishman, and the patriotic American rashly declared that you couldn't see a sunrise like that anywhere in Europe, and this gave the Irishman his chance, and he said, 'Sure ye don't have 'm here till we're through with 'em over there.' "

" It is true," said Dear Jones, thoughtfully, " that they do have some things over there better than we do ; for instance, umbrellas."

" And gowns," added the Duchess.

" And antiquities "—this was Uncle Larry's contribution.

" And we do have some things so much better in America!" protested Baby Van Rensselaer, as yet uncorrupted by any worship of the effete monarchies of despotic Europe. " We make lots of things a great deal nicer than you can get them in Europe—especially ice-cream."

"And pretty girls," added Dear Jones ; but he did not look at her.

"And spooks," remarked Uncle Larry, casually.

"Spooks ?" queried the Duchess.

"Spooks. I maintain the word. Ghost, if you like that better, or spectres. We turn out the best quality of spook—"

"You forget the lovely ghost stories about the Rhine and the Black Forest," interrupted Miss Van Rensselaer, with feminine inconsistency.

"I remember the Rhine and the Black Forest and all the other haunts of elves and fairies and hobgoblins ; but for good, honest spooks there is no place like home. And what differentiates our spook—*spiritus Americanus*—from the ordinary ghost of literature is that it responds to the American sense of humor. Take Irving's stories, for example. The 'Headless Horseman'—that's a comic ghost story. And Rip Van Winkle—consider what humor, and what good humor, there is in the telling of his meeting with the goblin crew of Hendrik Hudson's men ! A still better example of this American way of dealing

7

with legend and mystery is the marvellous tale of the rival ghosts."

"The rival ghosts!" queried the Duchess and Baby Van Rensselaer together. "Who were they?"

"Didn't I ever tell you about them?" answered Uncle Larry, a gleam of approaching joy flashing from his eye.

"Since he is bound to tell us sooner or later, we'd better be resigned and hear it now," said Dear Jones.

"If you are not more eager, I won't tell it at all."

"Oh, do, Uncle Larry! you know I just dote on ghost stories," pleaded Baby Van Rensselaer.

"Once upon a time," began Uncle Larry — "in fact, a very few years ago—there lived in the thriving town of New York a young American called Duncan—Eliphalet Duncan. Like his name, he was half Yankee and half Scotch, and naturally he was a lawyer, and had come to New York to make his way. His father was a Scotchman who had come over and settled in Boston and married a Salem girl. When Eliphalet Duncan was

about twenty he lost both of his parents.
His father left him enough money to give
him a start, and a strong feeling of pride in
his Scotch birth; you see there was a title in
the family in Scotland, and although Eliphalet's father was the younger son of a younger son, yet he always remembered, and always
bade his only son to remember, that this an-
cestry was noble. His mother left him her
full share of Yankee grit and a little old house
in Salem which had belonged to her family
for more than two hundred years. She was a
Hitchcock, and the Hitchcocks had been settled in Salem since the year 1. It was a great-
great-grandfather of Mr. Eliphalet Hitchcock
who was foremost in the time of the Salem
witchcraft craze. And this little old house
which she left to my friend Eliphalet Duncan
was haunted."

" By the ghost of one of the witches, of
course ?" interrupted Dear Jones.

" Now how could it be the ghost of a witch,
since the witches were all burned at the stake ?
You never heard of anybody who was burned
having a ghost, did you ?" asked Uncle Larry.

" That's an argument in favor of cremation,

at any rate," replied Dear Jones, evading the direct question.

"It is, if you don't like ghosts. I do," said Baby Van Rensselaer.

"And so do I," added Uncle Larry. "I love a ghost as dearly as an Englishman loves a lord."

"Go on with your story," said the Duchess, majestically overruling all extraneous discussion.

"This little old house at Salem was haunted," resumed Uncle Larry. "And by a very distinguished ghost—or at least by a ghost with very remarkable attributes."

"What was he like?" asked Baby Van Rensselaer, with a premonitory shiver of anticipatory delight.

"It had a lot of peculiarities. In the first place, it never appeared to the master of the house. Mostly it confined its visitations to unwelcome guests. In the course of the last hundred years it had frightened away four successive mothers-in-law, while never intruding on the head of the household."

"I guess that ghost had been one of the boys when he was alive and in the flesh."

This was Dear Jones's contribution to the telling of the tale.

"In the second place," continued Uncle Larry, "it never frightened anybody the first time it appeared. Only on the second visit were the ghost-seers scared; but then they were scared enough for twice, and they rarely mustered up courage enough to risk a third interview. One of the most curious characteristics of this well-meaning spook was that it had no face—or at least that nobody ever saw its face."

"Perhaps he kept his countenance veiled?" queried the Duchess, who was beginning to remember that she never did like ghost stories.

"That was what I was never able to find out. I have asked several people who saw the ghost, and none of them could tell me anything about its face, and yet while in its presence they never noticed its features, and never remarked on their absence or concealment. It was only afterwards when they tried to recall calmly all the circumstances of meeting with the mysterious stranger that they became aware that they had not seen its face. And they could not say whether the features were

covered, or whether they were wanting, or
what the trouble was. They knew only that
the face was never seen. And no matter how
often they might see it, they never fathomed
this mystery. To this day nobody knows
whether the ghost which used to haunt the
little old house in Salem had a face, or what
manner of face it had."

"How awfully weird!" said Baby Van
Rensselaer. "And why did the ghost go
away?"

"I haven't said it went away," answered
Uncle Larry, with much dignity.

"But you said it *used* to haunt the little old
house at Salem, so I supposed it had moved.
Didn't it?" the young lady asked.

"You shall be told in due time. Eliphalet
Duncan used to spend most of his summer va-
cations at Salem, and the ghost never bothered
him at all, for he was the master of the house
—much to his disgust, too, because he wanted
to see for himself the mysterious tenant at will
of his property. But he never saw it, never.
He arranged with friends to call him whenever it might appear, and he slept in the next
room with the door open; and yet when their

frightened cries waked him the ghost was
gone, and his only reward was to hear re-
proachful sighs as soon as he went back to
bed. You see, the ghost thought it was not
fair of Eliphalet to seek an introduction which
was plainly unwelcome."

Dear Jones interrupted the story-teller by
getting up and tucking a heavy rug more
snugly around Baby Van Rensselaer's feet, for
the sky was now overcast and gray, and the
air was damp and penetrating.

"One fine spring morning," pursued Uncle
Larry, "Eliphalet Duncan received great news.
I told you that there was a title in the family
in Scotland, and that Eliphalet's father was
the younger son of a younger son. Well, it
happened that all Eliphalet's father's brothers
and uncles had died off without male issue except the eldest son of the eldest son, and he, of
course, bore the title, and was Baron Duncan
of Duncan. Now the great news that Eliphalet Duncan received in New York one fine
spring morning was that Baron Duncan and
his only son had been yachting in the Hebrides, and they had been caught in a black
squall, and they were both dead. So my

friend Eliphalet Duncan inherited the title and the estates."

"How romantic!" said the Duchess. "So he was a baron!"

"Well," answered Uncle Larry, "he was a baron if he chose. But he didn't choose."

"More fool he!" said Dear Jones, sententiously.

"Well," answered Uncle Larry, "I'm not so sure of that. You see, Eliphalet Duncan was half Scotch and half Yankee, and he had two eyes to the main chance. He held his tongue about his windfall of luck until he could find out whether the Scotch estates were enough to keep up the Scotch title. He soon discovered that they were not, and that the late Lord Duncan, having married money, kept up such state as he could out of the revenues of the dowry of Lady Duncan. And Eliphalet, he decided that he would rather be a well-fed lawyer in New York, living comfortably on his practice, than a starving lord in Scotland, living scantily on his title."

"But he kept his title?" asked the Duchess.

"Well," answered Uncle Larry, "he kept it quiet. I knew it, and a friend or two more.

But Eliphalet was a sight too smart to put 'Baron Duncan of Duncan, Attorney and Counsellor at Law,' on his shingle."

"What has all this got to do with your ghost?" asked Dear Jones, pertinently.

"Nothing with that ghost, but a good deal with another ghost. Eliphalet was very learned in spirit lore—perhaps because he owned the haunted house at Salem, perhaps because he was a Scotchman by descent. At all events, he had made a special study of the wraiths and white ladies and banshees and bogies of all kinds whose sayings and doings and warnings are recorded in the annals of the Scottish nobility. In fact, he was acquainted with the habits of every reputable spook in the Scotch peerage. And he knew that there was a Duncan ghost attached to the person of the holder of the title of Baron Duncan of Duncan."

"So, besides being the owner of a haunted house in Salem, he was also a haunted man in Scotland?" asked Baby Van Rensselaer.

"Just so. But the Scotch ghost was not unpleasant, like the Salem ghost, although it had one peculiarity in common with its trans-

atlantic fellow-spook. It never appeared to
the holder of the title, just as the other never
was visible to the owner of the house. In
fact, the Duncan ghost was never seen at all.
It was a guardian angel only. Its sole duty
was to be in personal attendance on Baron
Duncan of Duncan, and to warn him of impending evil. The traditions of the house
told that the Barons of Duncan had again and
again felt a premonition of ill fortune. Some
of them had yielded and withdrawn from the
venture they had undertaken, and it had
failed dismally. Some had been obstinate,
and had hardened their hearts, and had gone
on reckless to defeat and to death. In no
case had a Lord Duncan been exposed to peril
without fair warning."

"Then how came it that the father and son
were lost in the yacht off the Hebrides?" asked
Dear Jones.

"Because they were too enlightened to
yield to superstition. There is extant now a
letter of Lord Duncan, written to his wife a
few minutes before he and his son set sail, in
which he tells her how hard he has had to
struggle with an almost overmastering desire

to give up the trip. Had he obeyed the
friendly warning of the family ghost, the
letter would have been spared a journey
across the Atlantic."

"Did the ghost leave Scotland for America
as soon as the old baron died?" asked Baby
Van Rensselaer, with much interest.

"How did he come over," queried Dear
Jones — "in the steerage, or as a cabin passenger?"

"I don't know," answered Uncle Larry,
calmly, "and Eliphalet didn't know. For as
he was in no danger, and stood in no need
of warning, he couldn't tell whether the ghost
was on duty or not. Of course he was on the
watch for it all the time. But he never got
any proof of its presence until he went down
to the little old house of Salem, just before
the Fourth of July. He took a friend down
with him—a young fellow who had been in
the regular army since the day Fort Sumter
was fired on, and who thought that after four
years of the little unpleasantness down South,
including six months in Libby, and after ten
years of fighting the bad Indians on the plains,
he wasn't likely to be much frightened by a

ghost.   Well, Eliphalet and the officer sat out
on the porch all the evening smoking and
talking over points in military law.   A little
after twelve o'clock, just as they began to
think it was about time to turn in, they heard
the most ghastly noise in the house.   It wasn't
a shriek, or a howl, or a yell, or anything they
could put a name to.   It was an undetermin-
ate, inexplicable shiver and shudder of sound,
which went wailing out of the window.   The
officer had been at Cold Harbor, but he felt
himself getting colder this time.   Eliphalet
knew it was the ghost who haunted the house.
As this weird sound died away, it was followed
by another, sharp, short, blood-curdling in its
intensity.   Something in this cry seemed familiar to Eliphalet, and he felt sure that it proceeded from the family ghost, the warning
wraith of the Duncans."

"Do I understand you to intimate that both
ghosts were there together?" inquired the
Duchess, anxiously.

"Both of them were there," answered Uncle
Larry.   "You see, one of them belonged to
the house, and had to be there all the time,
and the other was attached to the person of

Baron Duncan, and had to follow him there; wherever he was, there was that ghost also. But Eliphalet, he had scarcely time to think this out when he heard both sounds again, not one after another, but both together, and something told him—some sort of an instinct he had—that those two ghosts didn't agree, didn't get on together, didn't exactly hit it off; in fact, that they were quarrelling."

"Quarrelling ghosts! Well, I never!" was Baby Van Rensselaer's remark.

"It is a blessed thing to see ghosts dwell together in unity," said Dear Jones.

And the Duchess added, "It would certainly be setting a better example."

"You know," resumed Uncle Larry, "that two waves of light or of sound may interfere and produce darkness or silence. So it was with these rival spooks. They interfered, but they did not produce silence or darkness. On the contrary, as soon as Eliphalet and the officer went into the house, there began at once a series of spiritualistic manifestations—a regular dark séance. A tambourine was played upon, a bell was rung, and a flaming banjo went singing around the room."

"Where did they get the banjo?" asked Dear Jones, sceptically.

"I don't know. Materialized it, maybe, just as they did the tambourine. You don't suppose a quiet New York lawyer kept a stock of musical instruments large enough to fit out a strolling minstrel troupe just on the chance of a pair of ghosts coming to give him a surprise party, do you? Every spook has its own instrument of torture. Angels play on harps, I'm informed, and spirits delight in banjos and tambourines. These spooks of Eliphalet Duncan's were ghosts with all modern improvements, and I guess they were capable of providing their own musical weapons. At all events, they had them there in the little old house at Salem the night Eliphalet and his friend came down. And they played on them, and they rang the bell, and they rapped here, there, and everywhere. And they kept it up all night."

"All night?" asked the awe-stricken Duchess.

"All night long," said Uncle Larry, solemnly; "and the next night too. Eliphalet did not get a wink of sleep, neither did his friend. On

the second night the house ghost was seen by
the officer; on the third night it showed itself again; and the next morning the officer
packed his gripsack and took the first train to
Boston. He was a New-Yorker, but he said
he'd sooner go to Boston than see that ghost
again. Eliphalet wasn't scared at all, partly because he never saw either the domiciliary or the titular spook, and partly because
he felt himself on friendly terms with the
spirit world, and didn't scare easily. But after
losing three nights' sleep and the society of
his friend, he began to be a little impatient,
and to think that the thing had gone far
enough. You see, while in a way he was
fond of ghosts, yet he liked them best one at
a time. Two ghosts were one too many. He
wasn't bent on making a collection of spooks.
He and one ghost were company, but he and
two ghosts were a crowd."

"What did he do?" asked Baby Van Rensselaer.

"Well, he couldn't do anything. He waited
awhile, hoping they would get tired; but he
got tired out first. You see, it comes natural
to a spook to sleep in the daytime, but a man

wants to sleep nights, and they wouldn't let
him sleep nights. They kept on wrangling
and quarrelling incessantly; they manifested
and they dark-séanced as regularly as the old
clock on the stairs struck twelve; they rapped
and they rang bells and they banged the tambourine and they threw the flaming banjo
about the house, and, worse than all, they
swore."

"I did not know that spirits were addicted
to bad language," said the Duchess.

"How did he know they were swearing? Could he hear them?" asked Dear
Jones.

"That was just it," responded Uncle Larry;
"he could not hear them—at least, not distinctly. There were inarticulate murmurs and
stifled rumblings. But the impression pro-
duced on him was that they were swearing.
If they had only sworn right out, he would
not have minded it so much, because he would
have known the worst. But the feeling that
the air was full of suppressed profanity was
very wearing, and after standing it for a week
he gave up in disgust and went to the White
Mountains."

" Leaving them to fight it out, I suppose," interjected Baby Van Rensselaer.

" Not at all," explained Uncle Larry. " They could not quarrel unless he was present. You see, he could not leave the titular ghost behind him, and the domiciliary ghost could not leave the house. When he went away he took the family ghost with him, leaving the house ghost behind. Now spooks can't quarrel when they are a hundred miles apart any more than men can."

" And what happened afterwards ?" asked Baby Van Rensselaer, with a pretty impatience.

" A most marvellous thing happened. Eliphalet Duncan went to the White Mountains, and in the car of the railroad that runs to the top of Mount Washington he met a classmate whom he had not seen for years, and this classmate introduced Duncan to his sister, and this sister was a remarkably pretty girl, and Duncan fell in love with her at first sight, and by the time he got to the top of Mount Washington he was so deep in love that he began to consider his own unworthiness, and to wonder whether she might ever be induced to care for him a little—ever so little."

8

"I don't think that is so marvellous a thing," said Dear Jones, glancing at Baby Van Rensselaer.

"Who was she?" asked the Duchess, who had once lived in Philadelphia.

"She was Miss Kitty Sutton, of San Francisco, and she was a daughter of old Judge Sutton, of the firm of Pixley & Sutton."

"A very respectable family," assented the Duchess.

"I hope she wasn't a daughter of that loud and vulgar old Mrs. Sutton whom I met at Saratoga one summer four or five years ago?" said Dear Jones.

"Probably she was," Uncle Larry responded.

"She was a horrid old woman. The boys used to call her Mother Gorgon."

"The pretty Kitty Sutton with whom Eliphalet Duncan had fallen in love was the daughter of Mother Gorgon. But he never saw the mother, who was in Frisco, or Los Angeles, or Santa Fé, or somewhere out West, and he saw a great deal of the daughter, who was up in the White Mountains. She was travelling with her brother and his wife, and as they journeyed from hotel to hotel Duncan went with them, and filled out the quartette. Before the end of the summer he began to think about proposing. Of course he had lots of chances, going on excursions as they were every day. He made up his mind to seize the first opportunity, and that very evening he took her out for a moonlight row on Lake Winipiseogee. As he handed her into the boat he resolved to do it, and he had a glimmer of a suspicion that she knew he was going to do it, too."

"Girls," said Dear Jones, "never go out in a row-boat at night with a young man unless you mean to accept him."

"Sometimes it's best to refuse him, and get it over once for all," said Baby Van Rensselaer, impersonally.

"As Eliphalet took the oars he felt a sudden chill. He tried to shake it off, but in vain. He began to have a growing consciousness of impending evil. Before he had taken ten strokes—and he was a swift oarsman—he was aware of a mysterious presence between him and Miss Sutton."

"Was it the guardian-angel ghost warning him off the match?" interrupted Dear Jones.

"That's just what it was," said Uncle Larry. "And he yielded to it, and kept his peace, and rowed Miss Sutton back to the hotel with his proposal unspoken."

"More fool he," said Dear Jones. "It will take more than one ghost to keep me from proposing when my mind is made up." And he looked at Baby Van Rensselaer.

"The next morning," continued Uncle Larry, "Eliphalet overslept himself, and when he went down to a late breakfast he found that the Suttons had gone to New York by the morning train. He wanted to follow them at once, and again he felt the mysterious presence overpowering his will. He struggled two days, and at last he roused himself to do what he wanted in spite of the spook. When he arrived in New York it was late in the evening. He dressed himself hastily, and went to the hotel where the Suttons were, in the hope of seeing at least her brother. The guardian angel fought every inch of the walk with him, until he began to wonder whether, if Miss Sutton were to take him, the spook would forbid the banns. At the hotel he saw no one that night, and he went home determined to call as early as he

could the next afternoon, and make an end of
it. When he left his office about two o'clock
the next day to learn his fate, he had not
walked five blocks before he discovered that
the wraith of the Duncans had withdrawn his
opposition to the suit. There was no feeling
of impending evil, no resistance, no struggle,
no consciousness of an opposing presence.
Eliphalet was greatly encouraged. He walked
briskly to the hotel; he found Miss Sutton
alone. He asked her the question, and got his
answer."

"She accepted him, of course?" said Baby
Van Rensselaer.

"Of course," said Uncle Larry. "And while
they were in the first flush of joy, swapping
confidences and confessions, her brother came
into the parlor with an expression of pain on
his face and a telegram in his hand. The former was caused by the latter, which was from
Frisco, and which announced the sudden death
of Mrs. Sutton, their mother."

"And that was why the ghost no longer
opposed the match?" questioned Dear Jones.

"Exactly. You see, the family ghost knew
that Mother Gorgon was an awful obstacle to

Duncan's happiness, so it warned him. But the moment the obstacle was removed, it gave its consent at once."

The fog was lowering its thick, damp curtain, and it was beginning to be difficult to see from one end of the boat to the other. Dear Jones tightened the rug which enwrapped Baby Van Rensselaer, and then withdrew again into his own substantial coverings.

Uncle Larry paused in his story long enough to light another of the tiny cigars he always smoked.

"I infer that Lord Duncan"—the Duchess was scrupulous in the bestowal of titles—"saw no more of the ghosts after he was married."

"He never saw them at all, at any time, either before or since. But they came very near breaking off the match, and thus breaking two young hearts."

"You don't mean to say that they knew any just cause or impediment why they should not forever after hold their peace?" asked Dear Jones.

"How could a ghost, or even two ghosts, keep a girl from marrying the man she loved?" This was Baby Van Rensselaer's question.

"It seems curious, doesn't it?" and Uncle
Larry tried to warm himself by two or three
sharp pulls at his fiery little cigar. "And the
circumstances are quite as curious as the fact
itself. You see, Miss Sutton wouldn't be married for a year after her mother's death, so she
and Duncan had lots of time to tell each other all they knew. Eliphalet got to know a
good deal about the girls she went to school
with; and Kitty soon learned all about his
family. He didn't tell her about the title for
a long time, as he wasn't one to brag. But he
described to her the little old house at Salem.
And one evening towards the end of the summer, the wedding-day having been appointed
for early in September, she told him that she
didn't want a bridal tour at all; she just wanted
to go down to the little old house at Salem to
spend her honeymoon in peace and quiet, with
nothing to do and nobody to bother them.
Well, Eliphalet jumped at the suggestion: it
suited him down to the ground. All of a sudden he remembered the spooks, and it knocked
him all of a heap. He had told her about the
Duncan banshee, and the idea of having an
ancestral ghost in personal attendance on her

husband tickled her immensely. But he had
never said anything about the ghost which
haunted the little old house at Salem. He
knew she would be frightened out of her wits
if the house ghost revealed itself to her, and
he saw at once that it would be impossible to
go to Salem on their wedding trip. So he told
her all about it, and how whenever he went to
Salem the two ghosts interfered, and gave
dark séances and manifested and materialized
and made the place absolutely impossible.
Kitty listened in silence, and Eliphalet thought
she had changed her mind. But she hadn't
done anything of the kind."

"Just like a man—to think she was going
to," remarked Baby Van Rensselaer.

"She just told him she could not bear
ghosts herself, but she would not marry a
man who was afraid of them."

"Just like a girl—to be so inconsistent,"
remarked Dear Jones.

Uncle Larry's tiny cigar had long been ex-
tinct. He lighted a new one, and continued:
"Eliphalet protested in vain. Kitty said her
mind was made up. She was determined to
pass her honeymoon in the little old house at

Salem, and she was equally determined not to
go there as long as there were any ghosts there.
Until he could assure her that the spectral
tenant had received notice to quit, and that
there was no danger of manifestations and
materializing, she refused to be married at all.
She did not intend to have her honeymoon
interrupted by two wrangling ghosts, and the
wedding could be postponed until he had
made ready the house for her."

"She was an unreasonable young woman,"
said the Duchess.

"Well, that's what Eliphalet thought, much
as he was in love with her. And he believed
he could talk her out of her determination.
But he couldn't. She was set. And when a
girl is set, there's nothing to do but to yield
to the inevitable. And that's just what Eliphalet did. He saw he would either have to
give her up or to get the ghosts out; and as
he loved her and did not care for the ghosts,
he resolved to tackle the ghosts. He had
clear grit, Eliphalet had—he was half Scotch
and half Yankee, and neither breed turns tail
in a hurry. So he made his plans and he
went down to Salem. As he said good-bye to

Kitty he had an impression that she was sorry she had made him go; but she kept up bravely, and put a bold face on it, and saw him off, and went home and cried for an hour, and was perfectly miserable until he came back the next day."

"Did he succeed in driving the ghosts away?" asked Baby Van Rensselaer, with great interest.

"That's just what I'm coming to," said Uncle Larry, pausing at the critical moment, in the manner of the trained story-teller. "You see, Eliphalet had got a rather tough job, and he would gladly have had an extension of time on the contract, but he had to choose between the girl and the ghosts, and he wanted the girl. He tried to invent or remember some short and easy way with ghosts, but he couldn't. He wished that somebody had invented a specific for spooks—something that would make the ghosts come out of the house and die in the yard. He wondered if he could not tempt the ghosts to run in debt, so that he might get the sheriff to help him. He wondered also whether the ghosts could not be overcome with strong drink—a dissipated spook, a spook with delirium tremens, might be committed to the inebriate asylum. But none of these things seemed feasible."

" What did he do ?" interrupted Dear Jones. " The learned counsel will please speak to the point."

" You will regret this unseemly haste," said Uncle Larry, gravely, " when you know what really happened."

" What was it, Uncle Larry?" asked Baby Van Rensselaer. " I'm all impatience."

And Uncle Larry proceeded :

" Eliphalet went down to the little old house at Salem, and as soon as the clock struck twelve the rival ghosts began wrangling as before. Raps here, there, and everywhere, ringing bells, banging tambourines, strumming banjos sailing about the room, and all the other manifestations and materializations followed one another just as they had the summer before. The only difference Eliphalet could detect was a stronger flavor in the spectral profanity ; and this, of course, was only a vague impression, for he did not actually hear a single word. He waited awhile in patience, listening and watching. Of course he never saw either of the ghosts, because neither of them could appear to him. At last he got his dander up, and he thought it was about time to interfere, so he rapped on the table, and asked for silence. As soon as he felt that the spooks were listening to him he explained the situation to them. He told them he was in love, and that he could not marry unless they vacated the house. He appealed to them as old friends, and he laid claim to their gratitude. The titular ghost had been sheltered by the Duncan family for hundreds of years, and the domiciliary ghost had had free lodging in the little old house at Salem for nearly two centuries. He implored them to settle their differences, and to get him out of his difficulty at once. He suggested that they had better fight it out then and there, and see who was master. He had brought down with him all needful weapons. And he pulled out his valise, and spread on the table a pair of navy revolvers, a pair of shot-guns, a pair of duelling-swords, and a couple of bowie-knives. He offered to serve as second for both parties, and to give the word when to begin. He also took out of his valise a pack of cards and a

bottle of poison, telling them that if they
wished to avoid carnage they might cut the
cards to see which one should take the poison.
Then he waited anxiously for their reply.
For a little space there was silence. Then he
became conscious of a tremulous shivering in
one corner of the room, and he remembered
that he had heard from that direction what
sounded like a frightened sigh when he made
the first suggestion of the duel. Something
told him that this was the domiciliary ghost,
and that it was badly scared. Then he was
impressed by a certain movement in the opposite corner of the room, as though the
titular ghost were drawing himself up with
offended dignity. Eliphalet couldn't exactly
see those things, because he never saw the
ghosts, but he felt them. After a silence of
nearly a minute a voice came from the corner
where the family ghost stood—a voice strong
and full, but trembling slightly with suppressed passion. And this voice told Eliphalet
it was plain enough that he had not long been
the head of the Duncans, and that he had
never properly considered the characteristics
of his race if now he supposed that one of his

blood could draw his sword against a woman. Eliphalet said he had never suggested that the Duncan ghost should raise his hand against a woman, and all he wanted was that the Duncan ghost should fight the other ghost. And then the voice told Eliphalet that the other ghost was a woman."

"What?" said Dear Jones, sitting up suddenly. "You don't mean to tell me that the ghost which haunted the house was a woman?"

"Those were the very words Eliphalet Duncan used," said Uncle Larry; "but he did not need to wait for the answer. All at once he recalled the traditions about the domiciliary ghost, and he knew that what the titular ghost said was the fact. He had never thought of the sex of a spook, but there was no doubt whatever that the house ghost was a woman. No sooner was this firmly fixed in Eliphalet's mind than he saw his way out of the difficulty. The ghosts must be married!—for then there would be no more interference, no more quarrelling, no more manifestations and materializations, no more dark séances, with their raps and bells and tambourines and banjos. At first the ghosts would not hear of it. The

voice in the corner declared that the Duncan
wraith had never thought of matrimony. But
Eliphalet argued with them, and pleaded and
pursuaded and coaxed, and dwelt on the ad-
vantages of matrimony. He had to confess,
of course, that he did not know how to get a
clergyman to marry them; but the voice from
the corner gravely told him that there need be
no difficulty in regard to that, as there was no
lack of spiritual chaplains. Then, for the first
time, the house ghost spoke, a low, clear,
gentle voice, and with a quaint, old-fashioned
New England accent, which contrasted sharp-
ly with the broad Scotch speech of the family
ghost. She said that Eliphalet Duncan seemed
to have forgotten that she was married. But
this did not upset Eliphalet at all; he remembered the whole case clearly, and he told her
she was not a married ghost, but a widow,
since her husband had been hanged for murder-
ing her. Then the Duncan ghost drew attention to the great disparity in their ages, saying that he was nearly four hundred and fifty
years old, while she was barely two hundred.
But Eliphalet had not talked to juries for
nothing; he just buckled to, and coaxed those

ghosts into matrimony.   Afterwards he came
to the conclusion that they were willing to be
coaxed, but at the time he thought he had
pretty hard work to convince them of the ad-
vantages of the plan."

"Did he succeed?" asked Baby Van Rensselaer, with a woman's interest in matrimony.

"He did," said Uncle Larry. "He talked
the wraith of the Duncans and the spectre of
the little old house at Salem into a matrimoni-
al engagement. And from the time they were
engaged he had no more trouble with them.
They were rival ghosts no longer. They were
married by their spiritual chaplain the very
same day that Eliphalet Duncan met Kitty
Sutton in front of the railing of Grace Church.
The ghostly bride and bridegroom went away
at once on their bridal tour, and Lord and
Lady Duncan went down to the little old
house at Salem to pass their honeymoon."

Uncle Larry stopped. His tiny cigar was
out again. The tale of the rival ghosts was
told. A solemn silence fell on the little party
on the deck of the ocean steamer, broken
harshly by the hoarse roar of the fog-horn.

(1883.)

SIXTEEN YEARS WITHOUT A BIRTH-
DAY

SIXTEEN YEARS WITHOUT A BIRTH-DAY

HILE the journalist deftly dealt with the lobster *à la* Newburg, as it bubbled in the chafing-dish before him, the deep-toned bell of the church at the corner began to strike twelve.

"Give me your plates, quick," he said, "and we'll drink Jack's health before it's to-morrow."

The artist and the soldier and the professor of mathematics did as they were told ; and then they filled their glasses.

The journalist, still standing, looked the soldier in the eye, and said : "Jack, this is the first time The Quartet has met since the old school-days, ten years ago and more. That this reunion should take place on your birthday doubles the pleasure of the occasion. We wish you many happy returns of the day !"

Then the artist and the mathematician rose also, and they looked at the soldier, and repeated together, "Many happy returns of the day!"

Whereupon they emptied their glasses and sat down, and the soldier rose to his feet.

"Thank you, boys," he began, "but I think you have already made me enjoy this one birthday three times over. It was yesterday that I was twenty-six, and—"

"But I didn't meet you till last night," interrupted the journalist; "and yesterday was Sunday; and I couldn't get a box for the theatre and find the other half of The Quartet all on Sunday, could I?"

"I'm not complaining because yesterday was my real birthday," the soldier returned, "even if you have now protracted the celebration on to the third day—it's just struck midnight, you know. All I have to say is, that since you have given me a triplicate birthday this time, any future anniversary will have to spread itself over four days if it wants to beat the record, that's all." And he took his seat again.

"Well," said the artist, who had recently returned from Paris, "that won't happen till we see 'the week of the four Thursdays,' as the French say."

" And we sha'n't see that for a month of Sundays, I guess," the journalist rejoined.

There was a moment of silence, and then the mathematician spoke for the first time.

" A quadruplex birthday will be odd enough, I grant you," he began, " but I don't think it quite as remarkable as the case of the lady who had no birthday for sixteen years after she was born."

The soldier and the artist and the journalist all looked at the professor of mathematics, and they all smiled ; but his face remained perfectly grave.

" What's that you say ?" asked the journalist. " Sixteen years without a birthday ? Isn't that a very large order ?"

" Did you know the lady herself?" inquired the soldier.

" She was my grandmother," the mathematician answered. " She had no birthday for the first sixteen years of her life."

" You mean that she did not celebrate her birthdays, I suppose," the artist remarked. " That's nothing. I know lots of families where they don't keep any anniversaries at all."

"No," persisted the mathematician. "I meant what I said, and precisely what I said. My grandmother did not keep her first fifteen birthdays because she couldn't. She didn't have them to keep. They didn't happen. The first time she had a chance to celebrate her birthday was when she completed her sixteenth year —and I need not tell you that the family made the most of the event."

"This a real grandmother you are talking about," asked the journalist, "and not a fairy godmother?"

"I could understand her going without a birthday till she was four years old," the soldier suggested, "if she was born on the 29th of February."

"That accounts for four years," the mathematician admitted, "since my grandmother *was* born on the 29th of February."

"In what year?" the soldier pursued. "In 1796?"

The professor of mathematics nodded.

"Then that accounts for eight years," said the soldier.

"I don't see that at all," exclaimed the artist.

"It's easy enough," the soldier explained. "The year 1800 isn't a leap-year, you know. We have a leap-year every four years, except the final year of a century—1700, 1800, 1900."

"I didn't know that," said the artist.

"I'd forgotten it," remarked the journalist. "But that gets us over only half of the difficulty. He says his grandmother didn't have a birthday till she was sixteen. We can all see now how it was she went without this annual luxury for the first eight years. But who robbed her of the birthdays she was entitled to when she was eight and twelve. That's what I want to know."

"Born February 29, 1796, the Gregorian calendar deprives her of a birthday in 1800," the soldier said. "But she ought to have had her first chance February 29, 1804. I don't see how—" and he paused in doubt. "Oh!" he cried, suddenly; "where was she living in 1804?"

"Most of the time in Russia," the mathematician answered. "Although the family went to England for a few days early in the year."

"What was the date when they left Russia?" asked the soldier, eagerly.

"They sailed from St. Petersburg in a Russian bark on the 10th of February," answered the professor of mathematics, "and owing to head-winds they did not reach England for a fortnight."

"Exactly," cried the soldier. "That's what I thought. That accounts for it."

"I don't see how," the artist declared; "that is, unless you mean to suggest that the Czar confiscated the little American girl's birthday and sent it to Siberia."

"It's plain enough," the soldier returned. "We have the reformed calendar, the Gregorian calendar, you know, and the Russians haven't. They keep the old Julian calendar, and it's now ten days behind ours. They celebrate Christmas three days after we have begun the new year. So if the little girl left St. Petersburg in a Russian ship on February 10, 1804, by the old reckoning, and was on the water two weeks, she would land in England after March 1st by the new calendar."

"That is to say," the artist inquired, "the little girl came into an English port thinking she

LOST AGAIN

P. 136

was going to have her birthday the next week, and when she set foot on shore she found out that her birthday was passed the week before. Is that what you mean?"

"Yes," answered the soldier; and the mathematician nodded also.

"Then all I have to say," the artist continued, "is that it was a mean trick to play on a child that had been looking forward to her first birthday for eight years—to knock her into the middle of next week in that fashion!"

"And she had to go four years more for her next chance," said the journalist. "Then she would be twelve. But you said she hadn't a birthday till she was sixteen. How did she lose the one she was entitled to in 1808? She wasn't on a Russian ship again, was she?"

"No," the mathematician replied; "she was on an American ship that time."

"On the North Sea?" asked the artist.

"No," was the calm answer; "on the Pacific."

"Sailing east or west?" cried the soldier.

"Sailing east," answered the professor of mathematics, smiling again.

"Then I see how it might happen," the soldier declared.

" Well, I don't," confessed the artist.

The journalist said nothing, as it seemed un-professional to admit ignorance of anything.

" It is simple enough," the soldier explained. " You see, the world is revolving about the sun steadily, and it is always high noon somewhere on the globe.   The day rolls round unceasing, and it is not cut off into twenty-four hours. We happen to have taken the day of Green-wich or Paris as the day of civilization, and we say that it begins earlier in China and later in California; but it is all the same day, we say.   Therefore there has to be some place out in the middle of the Pacific Ocean where we lose or gain a day—if we are going east, we gain it; if we are going west, we lose it.   Now I suppose this little girl of twelve was on her way from some Asiatic port to some Ameri-can port, and they stopped on their voyage at Honolulu.   Perhaps they dropped anchor there just before midnight on their February 28, 1808, thinking that the morrow would be the 29th; but when they were hailed from the shore, just after midnight, they found out that it was already March 1st."

As the soldier finished, he looked at the

mathematician for confirmation of his explanation.

Thus appealed to, the professor of mathematics smiled and nodded, and said: " You have hit it. That's just how it was that my grandmother lost the birthday she ought to have had when she was twelve, and had to go four years more without one."

" And so she really didn't have a birthday till she was sixteen !" the artist observed. " Well, all I can say is, your great-grandfather took too many chances. I don't think he gave the child a fair show. I hope he made it up to her when she was sixteen—that's all !"

An hour later The Quartet separated. The soldier and the artist walked away together, but the journalist delayed the mathematician.

" I say," he began, " that yarn about your grandmother was very interesting. It is an extraordinary combination of coincidences. I can see it in the Sunday paper with a scarehead—

'SIXTEEN YEARS WITHOUT A BIRTHDAY !'
Do you mind my using it ?"

" But it isn't true," said the professor.

" Not true ?" echoed the journalist.

"No," replied the mathematician. "I made it up. I hadn't done my share of the talking, and I didn't want you to think I had nothing to say for myself."

"Not a single word of truth in it?" the journalist returned.

"Not a single word," was the mathematician's answer.

"Well, what of that?" the journalist declared. "I don't want to file it in an affidavit —I want to print it in a newspaper."

(1894.)

THE TWINKLING OF AN EYE

I

T HE telegraph messenger looked again at the address on the envelope in his hand, and then scanned the house before which he was standing. It was an old-fashioned building of brick, two stories high, with an attic above; and it stood in an old-fashioned part of lower New York, not far from the East River. Over the wide archway there was a small weather-worn sign, "Ramapo Steel and Iron Works;" and over the smaller door alongside was a still smaller sign, "Whittier, Wheatcroft & Co."

When the messenger-boy had made out the name, he opened this smaller door and entered the long, narrow store. Its sides and walls were covered with bins and racks containing sample steel rails and iron beams, and coils of wire of various sizes. Down at the end of the store were desks where several clerks and book-keepers were at work.

As the messenger drew near, a red-headed office-boy blocked the passage, saying, somewhat aggressively, "Well?"

"Got a telegram for Whittier, Wheatcroft & Co.," the messenger explained, pugnaciously thrusting himself forward.

"In there!" the office-boy returned, jerking his thumb over his shoulder towards the extreme end of the building, an extension, roofed with glass and separated by a glass screen from the space where the clerks were at work.

The messenger pushed open the glazed door of this private office, a bell jingled over his head, and the three occupants of the room looked up.

"Whittier, Wheatcroft & Co.?" said the messenger, interrogatively, holding out the yellow envelope.

"Yes," responded Mr. Whittier, a tall, handsome old gentleman, taking the telegram. "You sign, Paul."

The youngest of the three, looking like his

father, took the messenger's book, and, glancing at an old-fashioned clock which stood in the corner, he wrote the name of the firm and the hour of delivery. He was watching the messenger go out. IIis attention was suddenly called to subjects of more importance by a sharp exclamation from his father.

"Well, well, well," said the elder Whittier with his eyes fixed on the telegram he had just read. "This is very strange—very strange indeed!"

"What's strange?" asked the third occupant of the office, Mr. Wheatcroft, a short, stout, irascible-looking man with a shock of grizzly hair.

For all answer Mr. Whittier handed to Mr. Wheatcroft the thin slip of paper.

No sooner had the junior partner read the paper than he seemed angrier than was usual with him.

"Strange!" he cried. "I should think it was strange! confoundedly strange—and deuced unpleasant, too."

"May I see what it is that's so very strange?" asked Paul, picking up the despatch.

"Of course you may see it," growled Mr.

10

Wheatcroft; "and let us see what you can make of it."

The young man read the message aloud: "Deal off. Can get quarter cent better terms. Carkendale."

Then he read it again to himself. At last he said, "I confess I don't see anything so very mysterious in that. We've lost a contract, I suppose; but that must have happened lots of times before, hasn't it?"

"It's happened twice before, this fall," returned Mr. Wheatcroft, fiercely, "after our bid had been practically accepted and just before the signing of the final contract!"

"Let me explain, Wheatcroft," interrupted the elder Whittier, gently. "You must not expect my son to understand the ins and outs of this business as we do. Besides, he has only been in the office ten days."

"I don't expect him to understand," growled Wheatcroft. "How could he? I don't understand it myself!"

"Close that door, Paul," said Mr. Whittier. "I don't want any of the clerks to know what we are talking about. Here are the facts in the case, and I think you will admit that they are certainly curious: Twice this fall, and now a third time, we have been the lowest bidders for important orders, and yet, just before our bid was formally accepted, somebody has cut under us by a fraction of a cent and got the job. First we thought we were going to get the building of the Barataria Central's bridge over the Little Makintosh River, but in the end it was the Tuxedo Steel Company that got the contract. Then there was the order for the fifty thousand miles of wire for the Transcontinental Telegraph; we made an extraordinarily low estimate on that. We wanted the contract, and we threw off, not only our profit, but even allowances for office expenses; and yet five minutes before the last bid had to be in, the Tuxedo Company put in an offer only a hundred and twenty-five dollars less than ours. Now comes the telegram to-day. The Methuselah Life Insurance Company is going to put up a big building; we were asked to estimate on the steel framework. We wanted that work—times are hard and there is little doing, as you know, and we must get work for our men if we can. We meant to have this contract if we could. We offered to do it at

what was really actual cost of manufacture—
without profit, first of all, and then without
any charge at all for office expenses, for interest on capital, for depreciation of plant. The
vice-president of the Methuselah, the one who
attends to all their real estate, is Mr. Carkendale. He told me yesterday that our bid was
very low, and that we were certain to get the
contract. And now he sends me this." Mr.
Whittier picked up the telegram again.

"But if we were going to do it at actual cost
of manufacture," said the young man, "and
somebody else underbids us, isn't somebody
else losing money on the job?"

"That's no sort of satisfaction to our men,"
retorted Mr. Wheatcroft, cooking himself
before the fire. "Somebody else — confound
him!—will be able to keep his men together
and to give them the wages we want for our
men. Do you think somebody else is the
Tuxedo Company again?"

"What of it?" asked Mr. Whittier. "Surely
you don't suppose—"

"Yes, I do," interrupted Mr. Wheatcroft,
swiftly. "I do, indeed. I haven't been in
this business thirty years for nothing. I know

how hungry we get at all times for a big, fat contract; and I know we would any of us give a hundred dollars to the man who could tell us what our chief rival has bid. It would be the cheapest purchase of the year, too." .

"Come, come, Wheatcroft," said the elder Whittier; "you know we've never done anything of that sort yet, and I think you and I are too old to be tempted now."

"Nothing of the sort," snorted the fiery little man; "I'm open to temptation this very moment. If I could know what the Tuxedo people are going to bid on the new steel rails of the Springfield and Athens, I'd give a thousand dollars."

"If I understand you, Mr. Wheatcroft," Paul Whittier asked, "you are suggesting that there has been something done that is not fair?"

"That's just what I mean," Mr. Wheatcroft declared, vehemently.

"Do you mean to say that the Tuxedo people have somehow been made acquainted with our bids?" asked the young man.

"That's what I'm thinking now," was the sharp answer. "I can't think of anything else. For two months we haven't been successful

in getting a single one of the big contracts.
We've had our share of the little things, of
course, but they don't amount to much. The
big things that we really wanted have slipped
through our fingers. We've lost them by the
skin of our teeth every time. That isn't ac-
cident, is it? Of course not! Then there's
only one explanation—there's a leak in this
office somewhere."

"You don't suspect any of the clerks, do
you, Mr. Wheatcroft?" asked the elder Whittier, sadly.

"I don't suspect anybody in particular," returned the junior partner, brushing his hair
up the wrong way; "and I suspect everybody
in general. I haven't an idea who it is, but
it's somebody! It must be somebody—and
if it is somebody, I'll do my best to get that
somebody into the clutches of the law."

"Who makes up the bids on these important
contracts?" asked Paul.

"Wheatcroft and I," answered his father.
"The specifications are forwarded to the works,
and the engineers make their estimates of the
actual cost of labor and material. These estimates are sent to us here, and we add what-

ever we think best for interest, and for expenses, for wear and tear, and for profit."

"Who writes the letters making the offer—
the one with actual figures I mean?" the son
continued.

"I do," the elder Whittier explained; "I
have always done it."

"You don't dictate them to a typewriter?"
Paul pursued.

"Certainly not," the father responded; "I
write them with my own hand, and, what's
more, I take the press-copy myself, and there
is a special letter-book for such things. This
letter-book is always kept in the safe in this
office; in fact, I can say that this particular
letter-book never leaves my hands except to
go into that safe. And, as you know, nobody
has access to that safe except Wheatcroft and
me."

"And the Major," corrected the junior
partner.

"No," Mr. Whittier explained, "Van Zandt
has no need to go there now."

"But he used to," Mr. Wheatcroft persisted.

"He did once," the senior partner returned;
"but when we bought those new safes outside

there in the main office, there was no longer any need for the chief book-keeper to go to this smaller safe; and so, last month—it was while you were away, Wheatcroft—Van Zandt came in here one afternoon, and said that, as he never had occasion to go to this safe, he would rather not have the responsibility of knowing the combination. I told him we had perfect confidence in him."

"I should think so!" broke in the explosive Wheatcroft. "The Major has been with us for thirty years now. I'd suspect myself of petty larceny as soon as him."

"As I said," continued the elder Whittier; "I told him that we trusted him perfectly, of course. But he urged me, and to please him I changed the combination of this safe that afternoon. You will remember, Wheatcroft, that I gave you the new word the day you came back."

"Yes, I remember," said Mr. Wheatcroft. "But I don't see why the Major did not want to know how to open that safe. Perhaps he is beginning to feel his years now. He must be sixty, the Major; and I've been thinking for some time that he looks worn."

"I noticed the change in him," Paul remarked, "the first day I came into the office. He seemed ten years older than he was last winter."

"Perhaps his wound troubles him again," suggested Mr. Whittier. "Whatever the reason, it is at his own request that he is now ignorant of the combination. No one knows that but Wheatcroft and I. The letters themselves I wrote myself, and copied myself, and put them myself in the envelopes I directed myself. I don't recall mailing them myself, but I may have done that too. So you see that there can't be any foundation for your belief, Wheatcroft, that somebody had access to our bids."

"I can't believe anything else!" cried Wheatcroft, impulsively. "I don't know how it was done—I'm not a detective—but it was done somehow. And if it was done, it was done by somebody! And what I'd like to do is to catch that somebody in the act—that's all! I'd make it hot for him!"

"You would like to have him out at the Ramapo Works," said Paul, smiling at the little man's violence, "and put him under the steam-hammer?"

"Yes, I would," responded Mr. Wheatcroft. "I would indeed! Putting a man under a steam-hammer may seem a cruel punishment, but I think it would cure the fellow of any taste for prying into our business in the future."

"I think it would get him out of the habit of living," the elder Whittier said, as the tall clock in the corner struck one. "But don't let's be so brutal. Let's go to lunch and talk the matter over quietly. I don't agree with your suspicion, Wheatcroft, but there may be something in it."

Five minutes later Mr. Whittier, Mr. Wheatcroft, and the only son of the senior partner left the glass-framed private office, and, walking leisurely through the long store, passed into the street.

They did not notice that the old book-keeper, Major Van Zandt, whose high desk was so placed that he could overlook the private office, had been watching them ever since the messenger had delivered the despatch. He could not read the telegram, he could not hear the comments, but he could see every movement and every gesture and every expression. He gazed from one speaker to the other almost as though he were able to follow the course of the discussion; and when the three members of the firm walked past his desk, he found himself staring at them as if in a vain effort to read on their faces the secret of the course of action they had resolved upon.

II

AFTER luncheon, as it happened, both the senior and the junior partner of Whittier, Wheatcroft & Co. had to attend meetings, and they went their several ways, leaving Paul to return to the office alone.

When he came opposite to the house which bore the weather-beaten sign of the firm he stood still for a moment, and looked across with mingled pride and affection. The building was old-fashioned—so old-fashioned, indeed, that only a long-established firm could afford to occupy it. It was Paul Whittier's great-grandfather who had founded the Ramapo Works. There had been cast the cannon for many of the ships of the little American navy that gave so good an account of itself in the war of 1812. Again, in 1848, had the house of Whittier, Wheatcroft & Co. — the present Mr. Wheatcroft's father having been taken into partnership by Paul's grandfather

—been able to be of service to the government
of the United States. All through the four
years that followed the firing on the flag in
1861 the Ramapo Works had been run day
and night. When peace came at last and the
people had leisure to expand, a large share of
the rails needed by the new overland roads
which were to bind the East and West together in iron bonds had been rolled by Whittier, Wheatcroft & Co. Of late years, as Paul
knew, the old firm seemed to have lost some
of its early energy, and, having young and
vigorous competitors, it had barely held its
own.

That the Ramapo Works should once more
take the lead was Paul Whittier's solemn purpose, and to this end he had been carefully
trained. He was now a young man of twenty-five, a tall, handsome fellow, with a full
mustache over his firm mouth, and with clear,
quick eyes below his curly brown hair. He
had spent four years in college, carrying off
honors in mathematics, was popular with his
classmates, who made him class poet, and in
his senior year he was elected president of the
college photographic society. He had gone to

a technological institute, where he had made himself master of the theory and practice of metallurgy. After a year of travel in Europe, where he had investigated all the important steel and iron works he could get into, he had come home to take a desk in the office.

It was only for a moment that he stood on the sidewalk opposite, looking at the old building. Then he threw away his cigarette and went over. Instead of entering the long store he walked down the alleyway left open for the heavy wagons. When he came opposite to the private office in the rear of the store he examined the doors and the windows carefully, to see if he could detect any means of ingress other than those open to everybody.

There was no door from the private office into the alleyway or into the yard. There was a door from the alleyway into the store, opposite to the desks of the clerks, and within a few feet of the door leading from the store into the private office.

Paul passed through this entrance, and found himself face to face with the old book-keeper, Van Zandt, who was following all his movements with a questioning gaze.

"Good-afternoon, Major," said Paul, pleasantly. "Have you been out for your lunch yet?"

"I always get my dinner at noon," the book-keeper gruffly answered, returning to his books.

As Paul walked on he could not but think that the Major's manner was ungracious. And the young man remembered how cheerful the old man had been, and how courteous always, when the son of the senior partner, while still a school-boy, used to come to the office on Saturdays.

Paul had always delighted in the office, and the store, and the yard behind, and he had spent many a holiday there, and Major Van Zandt had always been glad to see him, and had willingly answered his myriad questions.

Paul wondered why the book-keeper's manner was now so different. Van Zandt was older, but he was not so very old, not more than sixty, and old age in itself is not sufficient to make a man surly and to sour his temper. That the Major had had trouble in his family was well known. His wife had been flighty and foolish, and it was believed that she had run away from him; and his only son was a wild lad, who had been employed by Whittier, Wheatcroft & Co., out of regard for the father, and who had disgraced himself beyond forgiveness.   Paul recalled vaguely that the young fellow had gone West somewhere, and had been shot in a mining-camp after a drunken brawl in a gambling-house.

As Paul entered the private office he found the porter there, putting coal on the fire.

Stepping back to close the glass door behind him, that they might be alone, he said:

"Mike, who shuts up the office at night?"

"Sure I do, Mr. Paul," was the prompt reply.

"And you open it in the morning?" the young man asked.

"I do that!" Mike responded.

"Do you see that these windows are always fastened on the inside?" was the next query.

"Yes, Mr. Paul," the porter replied.

"Well," and the inquirer hesitated briefly before putting this question, "have you found any of these windows unfastened any morning lately when you came here?"

"And how did you know that?" Mike returned, in surprise.

"What morning was it?" asked Paul, pushing his advantage.

"It was last Monday mornin', Mr. Paul," the porter explained, "an' how it was I dunno, for I had every wan of them windows tight on Saturday night, an' Monday mornin' one of them was unfastened whin I wint to open it to let a bit of air into the office here."

"You sleep here always, don't you?" Paul proceeded.

"I've slept here ivery night for three years now come Thanksgivin'," Mike replied. "I've the whole top of the house to myself. It's an illigant apartment I have there, Mr. Paul."

"Who was here Sunday?" was the next question.

"Sure nobody was here at all," responded the porter, "barrin' they came while I took me a bit of a walk after dinner. An' they couldn't have got in anyway, for I lock up always, and I wasn't gone for an hour, or maybe an hour an' a half."

"I hope you will be very careful hereafter," said Paul.

11

"I will that," promised Mike, "an' I am careful now always."

The porter took up the coal-scuttle, and then he turned to Paul.

"How was it ye knew that the winder was not fastened that mornin'?" he asked.

"How did I know?" repeated the young man. "Oh, a little bird told me."

When Mike had left the office Paul took a chair before the fire and lighted a cigar. For half an hour he sat silently thinking.

He came to the conclusion that Mr. Wheatcroft was right in his suspicion. Whittier, Wheatcroft & Co. had lost important contracts because of underbidding, due to knowledge surreptitiously obtained. He believed that some one had got into the store on Sunday while Mike was taking a walk, and that this somebody had somehow opened the safe. There never was any money in that private safe; it was intended to contain only important papers. It did contain the letter-book of the firm's bids, and this is what was wanted by the man who had got into the office, and who had let himself in by the window, leaving it unfastened behind him. How this man

had got in, and why he did not get out by the
way he entered, how he came to be able to
open the private safe, the combination of
which was known only to the two partners—
these were questions for which Paul Whittier
had no answer.

What grieved him when he had come to the
conclusion was that the thief — for such the
house-breaker was in reality—was probably
one of the men in the employ of the firm. It
seemed to him almost certain that the man
who had broken in knew all the ins and outs
of the office. And how could this knowledge
have been obtained except by an employee?
Paul was well acquainted with the clerks in
the outer office. There were five of them, including the old book-keeper, and although
none of them had been with the firm as long
as the Major, no one of them had been there
less than ten years. Paul did not know which
one to suspect. There was, in fact, no reason
to suspect any particular clerk. And yet that
one of the five men in the main office on the
other side of the glass partition within twenty
feet of him—that one of these was the guilty
man Paul did not doubt.

And therefore it seemed to him not so important to prevent the thing from happening
again as it was to catch the man who had done
it.   The thief once caught, it would be easy
thereafter for the firm to take unusual pre-
cautions.   But the first thing to do was to
catch the thief.   He had come and gone, and
left no trail.   But he must have visited the
office at least three time in the past few weeks,
since the firm had lost three important contracts.   Probably he had been there oftener
than three times.   Certainly he would come
again.   Sooner or later he would come once
too often.   All that needed to be done was to
set a trap for him.

While Paul was sitting quietly in the private
office, smoking a cigar with all his mental fac-
ulties at their highest tension, the clock in the
corner suddenly struck three.

Paul swiftly swung around in his chair and
looked at it.   An old eight-day clock it was,
which not only told the time of the day, but
pretended, also, to supply miscellaneous astro-
nomical information.   It stood by itself in the
corner.

For a moment after it struck Paul stared at

it with a fixed gaze, as though he did not see what he was looking at. Then a light came into his eyes and a smile flitted across his lips.

He turned around slowly and measured with his eye the proportions of the room, the distance between the desks and the safe and the clock. He glanced up at the sloping glass roof above him. Then he smiled again, and again sat silent for a minute. He rose to his feet and stood with his back to the fire. Almost in front of him was the clock in the corner.

He took out his watch and compared its time with that of the clock. Apparently he found that the clock was too fast, for he walked over to it and turned the minute-hand back. It seemed that this was a more difficult feat than he supposed or that he went about it carelessly, for the minute-hand broke off ·short in his fingers. A spasmodic movement of his, as the thin metal snapped, pulled the chain off its cylinder, and the weight fell with a crash.

All the clerks looked up; and the red-headed office-boy was prompt in answer to the bell Paul rang a moment after.

"Bobby," said the young man to the boy,

as he took his hat and overcoat, "I've just broken the clock. I know a shop where they make a specialty of repairing timepieces like that. I'm going to tell them to send for it at once. Give it to the man who will come this afternoon with my card. Do you understand ?"

"Cert," the boy answered. "If he 'ain't got your card, he don't get the clock."

"That's what I mean," Paul responded, as he left the office.

Before he reached the door he met Mr. Wheatcroft.

"Paul," cried the junior partner, explosively, "I've been thinking about that—about that—you know what I mean! And I have decided that we had better put a detective on this thing at once !"

"Yes," said Paul, "that's a good idea. In fact, I had just come to the same conclusion. I—"

Then he checked himself. He had turned round slightly to speak to Mr. Wheatcroft; he saw that Major Van Zandt was standing within ten feet of them, and he noticed that the old book-keeper's face was strangely pale.

III

DURING the next week the office of Whittier, Wheatcroft & Co. had its usual aspect of prosperous placidity. The routine work was done in the routine way; the porter opened the office every morning, and the office-boy arrived a few minutes after it was opened; the clerks came at nine, and a little later the partners were to be seen in the inner office reading the morning's correspondence.

The Whittiers, father and son, had had a discussion with Mr. Wheatcroft as to the most advisable course to adopt to prevent the future leakage of the trade secrets of the firm. The senior partner had succeeded in dissuading the junior partner from the employment of detectives.

"Not yet," he said, "not yet. These clerks have all served us faithfully for years, and I don't want to submit them to the indignity of being shadowed—that's what they call it, isn't it?—of being shadowed by some cheap hireling who may try to distort the most innocent acts into evidence of guilt, so that he can show us how smart he is."

"But this sort of thing can't go on forever," ejaculated Mr. Wheatcroft. "If we are to be underbid on every contract worth having, we might as well go out of the business!"

"That's true, of course," Mr. Whittier admitted; "but we are not sure that we are being underbid unfairly."

"The Tuxedo Company have taken away three contracts from us in the past two months," cried the junior partner; "we can be sure of that, can't we?"

"We have lost three contracts, of course," returned Mr. Whittier, in his most conciliatory manner, "and the Tuxedo people have captured them. But that may be only a coincidence, after all."

"It is a pretty expensive coincidence for us," snorted Mr. Wheatcroft.

"But because we have lost money," the senior partner rejoined gently, laying his hand on Mr. Wheatcroft's arm, "that's no reason why we should also lose our heads. It is no reason why we should depart from our old custom of treating every man fairly. If there is any one in our employ here who is selling us, why, if we give him rope enough he will hang himself, sooner or later."

"And before he suspends himself that way," cried Mr. Wheatcroft, "we may be forced to suspend ourselves."

"Come, come, Wheatcroft," said the senior partner, "I think we can afford to stand the loss a little longer. What we can't afford to do is to lose our self-respect by doing something irreparable. It may be that we shall have to employ detectives, but I don't think the time has come yet."

"Very well," the junior partner declared, yielding an unwilling consent. "I don't insist on it. I still think it would be best not to waste any more time—but I don't insist. What will happen is that we shall lose the rolling of those steel rails for the Springfield and Athens road—that's all."

Paul Whittier had taken no part in this discussion. He agreed with his father, and saw he had no need to urge any further argument.

Presently he asked when they intended to

put in the bid for the rails. His father then explained that they were expecting a special estimate from the engineers at the Ramapo Works, and that it probably would be Saturday before this could be discussed by the partners and the exact figures of the proposed contract determined.

"And if we don't want to lose that contract for sure," insisted Mr. Wheatcroft, "I think we had better change the combination on that safe."

"May I suggest," said Paul, "that it seems to me to be better to leave the combination as it is. What we want to do is not to get this Springfield and Athens contract so much as to find out whether some one really is getting at the letter-book. Therefore we mustn't make it any harder for the some one to get at the letter-book."

"Oh, very well," Mr. Wheatcroft assented, a little ungraciously, "have it your own way. But I want you to understand now that I think you are only postponing the inevitable!"

And with that the subject was dropped. For several days the three men who were together for hours in the office of the Ramapo

Iron and Steel Works refrained from any discussion of the question which was most prominent in their minds.

It was on Wednesday that the tall clock that Paul Whittier had broken returned from the repairer's. Paul himself helped the men to set it in its old place in the corner of the office, facing the safe, which occupied the corner diagonally opposite.

It so chanced that Paul came down late on Thursday morning, and perhaps this was the reason that a pressure of delayed work kept him in the office that evening long after every one else. The clerks had all gone, even Major Van Zandt, always the last to leave— and the porter had come in twice before the son of the senior partner was ready to go for the night. The gas was lighted here and there in the long, narrow, deserted store, as Paul walked through it from the office to the street. Opposite, the swift twilight of a New York November had already settled down on the city.

"Can't I carry yer bag for ye, Mister Paul?" asked the porter, who was showing him out.

"No, thank you, Mike," was the young

man's answer. "That bag has very little in it. And, besides, I haven't got to carry it far."

The next morning Paul was the first of the three to arrive. The clerks were in their places already, but neither the senior nor the junior partner had yet come. The porter happened to be standing under the wagon archway as Paul Whittier was about to enter the store.

The young man saw the porter, and a mischievous smile hovered about the corners of his mouth.

"Mike," he said, pausing on the door-step, "do you think you ought to smoke while you are cleaning out our office in the morning?"

"Sure, I haven't had me pipe in me mouth this mornin' at all," the porter answered, taken by surprise.

"But yesterday morning?" Paul pursued.

"Yesterday mornin'!" Mike echoed, not a little puzzled.

"Yesterday morning at ten minutes before eight you were in the private office smoking a pipe."

"But how did you see me, Mr. Paul?" cried Mike, in amaze. "Ye was late in comin' down yesterday, wasn't ye?"

Paul smiled pleasantly.

"A little bird told me," he said.

"If I had the bird I'd ring his neck for tellin' tales," the porter remarked.

"I don't mind your smoking, Mike," the young man went on, "that's your own affair; but I'd rather you didn't smoke a pipe while you are tidying up the private office."

"Well, Mister Paul, I won't do it again," the porter promised.

"And I wouldn't encourage Bob to smoke, either," Paul continued.

"I encourage him?" inquired Mike.

"Yes," Paul explained; "yesterday morning you let him light his cigarette from your pipe—didn't you?"

"Were you peekin' in thro' the winder, Mister Paul?" the porter asked, eagerly. "Ye saw me, an' I never saw ye at all."

"No," the young man answered, "I can't say that I saw you myself. A little bird told me."

And with that he left the wondering porter and entered the store. Just inside the door was the office-boy, who hastily hid an unlighted cigarette as he caught sight of the senior partner's son.

When Paul saw the red-headed boy he smiled again, mischievously.

"Bob," he began, "when you want to see who can stand on his head the longest, you or Danny the boot-black, don't you think you could choose a better place than the private office?"

The office-boy was quite as much taken by surprise as the porter had been, but he was younger and quicker-witted.

"And when did I have Danny in the office?" he asked, defiantly.

"Yesterday morning," Paul answered, still smiling, "a little before half-past eight."

"Yesterday mornin'?" repeated Bob, as though trying hard to recall all the events of the day before. "Maybe Danny did come in for a minute."

"He played leap-frog with you all the way into the private office," Paul went on, while Bob looked at him with increasing wonder.

"How did you know?" the office-boy asked, frankly. "Were you lookin' through the window?"

"How do I know that you and Danny stood on your heads in the corner of the office with your heels against the safe, scratching off the paint? Next time I'd try the yard, if I were you. Sports of that sort are more fun in the open air."

And with that parting shot Paul went on his way to his own desk, leaving the office-boy greatly puzzled.

Later in the day Bob and Mike exchanged confidences, and neither was ready with an explanation.

"At school," Bob declared, "we used to think teacher had eyes in the back of her head. She was everlastingly catchin' me when I did things behind her back. But Mr. Paul beats that, for he see me doin' things when he wasn't here."

"Mister Paul wasn't here, for sure, yesterday mornin'," Mike asserted; "I'd take me oath o' that. An' if he wasn't here, how could he see me givin' ye a light from me pipe? Answer me that! He says it's a little bird told him; but that's not it, I'm thinkin'. Not but that they have clocks with birds into 'em, that come out and tell the time o' day, 'Cuckoo! Cuckoo! Cuckoo!' An' if that big clock he broke last week had a bird in it that could tell time that way, I'd break the thing quick—so I would."

"It ain't no bird," said Bob. "You can bet your life on that. No birds can't tell him nothin' no more'n you can catch 'em by putting salt on their tails. I know what it is Mr. Paul does—least, I know how he does it. It's second-sight, that's what it is! I see a man onct at the theayter, an' he—"

But perhaps it is not necessary to set down here the office-boy's recollection of the trick of an ingenious magician.

About half an hour after Paul had arrived at the office Mr. Wheatcroft appeared. The junior partner hesitated in the doorway for a second, and then entered.

Paul was watching him, and the same mischievous smile flashed over the face of the young man.

"You need not be alarmed to-day, Mr. Wheatcroft," he said. "There is no fascinating female waiting for you this morning."

"Confound the woman!" ejaculated Mr. Wheatcroft, testily. "I couldn't get rid of her."

"But you subscribed for the book at last," asserted Paul, "and she went away happy."

"I believe I did agree to take one copy of the work she showed me," admitted Mr. Wheatcroft, a little sheepishly. Then he looked up suddenly. "Why, bless my soul," he cried, "that was yesterday morning—"

"Allowing for differences of clocks," Paul returned, "it was about ten minutes to ten yesterday morning."

"Then how do you come to know anything about it? I should like to be told that!" the junior partner inquired. "You did not get down till nearly twelve."

"I had an eye on you," Paul answered, as the smile again flitted across his face.

"But I thought you were detained all the morning by a sick friend," insisted Mr. Wheatcroft.

"So I was," Paul responded. "And if you won't believe I had an eye on you, all I can say then is that a little bird told me."

"Stuff and nonsense!" cried Mr. Wheatcroft. "Your little bird has two legs, hasn't it?"

"Most birds have," laughed Paul.

"I mean two legs in a pair of trousers," explained the junior partner, rumpling his grizzled hair with an impatient gesture.

12

" You see how uncomfortable it is to be shadowed," said Paul, turning the topic as his father entered the office.

That Saturday afternoon Mr. Whittier and Mr. Wheatcroft agreed on the bid to be made on the steel rails needed by the Springfield and Athens road. While the elder Mr. Whittier wrote the letter to the railroad with his own hand, his son manœuvred the junior partner into the outer office, where all the clerks happened to be at work, including the old book-keeper. Then Paul managed his conversation with Mr. Wheatcroft so that any one of the five employees who chose to listen to the apparently careless talk should know that the firm had just made a bid on another important contract. Paul also spoke as though his father and himself would probably go out of town that Saturday night, to remain away till Monday morning.

And just before the store was closed for the night, Paul Whittier wound up the eight-day clock that stood in the corner opposite the private safe.

IV

ALTHOUGH the Whittiers, father and son, spent Sunday out of town, Paul made an excuse to the friends whom they were visiting, and returned to the city by a midnight train. Thus he was enabled to present himself at the office of the Ramapo Works very early on Monday morning.

It was so early, indeed, that no one of the employees had arrived when the son of the senior partner, bag in hand, pushed open the street door and entered the long store, at the far end of which the porter was still tidying up for the day's work.

"An' is that you, Mister Paul?" Mike asked in surprise, as he came out of the private office to see who the early visitor might be. "An' what brought ye out o' your bed before breakfast like this?"

"I always get out of bed before breakfast," Paul replied. "Don't you?"

"Would I get up if I hadn't got to get up to get my livin'?" the porter replied.

Paul entered the office, followed by Mike, still wondering why the young man was there at that hour.

After a swift glance round the office Paul put down his bag on the table and turned suddenly to the porter with a question.

"When does Bob get down here?"

Mike looked at the clock in the corner before answering.

"It 'll be ten minutes," he said, " or maybe twenty, before the boy does be here to-day, seein' it's Monday mornin', an' he'll be tired with not workin' of Sunday."

"Ten minutes," repeated Paul, slowly. After a moment's thought he continued, "Then I'll have to ask you to go out for me, Mike."

"I can go anywhere ye want, Mister Paul," the porter responded.

"I want you to go—" began Paul, "I want you to go—" and he hesitated, as though he was not quite sure what it was he wished the porter to do, "I want you to go to the office of the *Gotham Gazette* and get me two copies of yesterday's paper. Do you understand?"

"Maybe they won't be open so early in the mornin'," said the Irishman.

"That's no matter," said Paul, hastily correcting himself; "I mean that I want you to go there now and get the papers if you can. Of course, if the office isn't open I shall have to send again later."

"I'll be goin' now, Mister Paul," and Mike took his hat from a chair and started off at once.

Paul walked through the store with the porter. When Mike had gone the young man locked the front door and returned at once to the private office in the rear. He shut himself in, and lowered all the shades so that whatever he might do inside could not be seen by any one on the outside.

Whatever it was he wished to do he was able to do it swiftly, for in less than a minute after he had closed the door of the office he opened it again and came out into the main store with his bag in his hand. He walked leisurely to the front of the store, arriving just in time to unlock the door as the office-boy came around the corner smoking a cigarette.

When Bob, still puffing steadily, was about

to open the door and enter the store he looked up and discovered that Paul was gazing at him. The boy pinched the cigarette out of his mouth and dropped it outside, and then came in, his eyes expressing his surprise at the presence of the senior partner's son down-town at that early hour in the morning.

Paul greeted the boy pleasantly, but Bob got away from him as soon as possible. Ever since the young man had told what had gone on in the office when Bob was its only occupant, the office-boy was a little afraid of the young man, as though somewhat mysterious, not to say uncanny.

Paul thought it best to wait for the porter's return, and he stood outside under the archway for five minutes, smoking a cigar, with his bag at his feet.

When Mike came back with the two copies of the Sunday newspaper he had been sent to get, Paul gave him the money for them and an extra quarter for himself. Then the young man picked up his bag again.

"When my father comes down, Mike," he said, "tell him I may be a little late in getting back this morning."

" An' are ye goin' away now, Mister Paul ?" the porter asked. " What good was it that ye got out o' bed before breakfast and come down here so early in the mornin' ?"

Paul laughed a little. " I had a reason for coming here this morning," he answered, briefly ; and with that he walked away, his bag in one hand and the two bulky, gaudy papers in the other.

Mike watched him turn the corner, and then went into the store again, where Bob greeted him promptly with the query why the old man's son had been getting up by the 'bright light.

" If I was the boss, or the boss's son either," said Bob, " I wouldn't get up till I was good and ready. I'd have my breakfast in bed if I had a mind to, an' my dinner too, an' my supper. An' I wouldn't do no work, an' I'd go to the theayter every night, and twice on Saturdays."

" I dunno why Mister Paul was down," Mike explained. " All he wanted was two o' thim Sunday papers with pictures in thim. What did he want two o' thim for I dunno. There's reading enough in one o' thim to last me a month of Sundays."

It may be surmised that Mike would have been still more in the dark as to Paul Whittier's reasons for coming down-town so early that Monday morning if he could have seen the young man throw the copies of the *Gotham Gazette* into the first ash-cart he passed after he was out of range of the porter's vision.

Paul was not the only member of Whittier, Wheatcroft & Co. to arrive at the office early that morning. Mr. Wheatcroft was usually punctual, taking his seat at his desk just as the clock struck half-past nine. On this Monday morning he entered the store a little before nine.

As he walked back to the office he looked over at the desks of the clerks as though he was seeking some one.

At the door of the office he met Bob.

"Hasn't the Major come down yet?" he asked, shortly.

"No, sir," the boy answered. "He don't never get here till nine."

"H'm," grunted the junior partner. "When he does come, tell him I want to see him at once—at once, do you understand?"

" I ain't deaf and dumb and blind," Bob responded. " I'll steer him into you as soon as ever he shows up."

But, for a wonder, the old book-keeper was late that morning. Ordinarily he was a model of exactitude. Yet the clock struck nine, and half-past, and ten before he appeared in the store.

Before he changed his coat Bob was at his side.

" Mr. Wheatcroft he wants to see you now in a hurry," said the boy.

Major Van Zandt paled swiftly, and steadied himself by a grasp of the railing.

" Does Mr. Wheatcroft wish to see me ?" he asked, faintly.

" You bet he does," the boy answered, " an' in a hurry, too. He came bright an' early this morning a-purpose to see you, an' he's been a-waiting for two hours. An' I guess he's got his mad up now."

When the old book-keeper with his blanched face and his faltering step entered the private office Mr. Wheatcroft wheeled around in his chair.

" Oh, it's you, is it ?" he cried. " At last !"

"I regret that I was late this morning, Mr. Wheatcroft," Van Zandt began.

"That's no matter," said the employer;— "at least, I want to talk about something else."

"About something else?" echoed the old man, feebly.

"Yes," responded Mr. Wheatcroft. "Shut the door behind you, please, so that that red-headed cub out there can't hear what I am going to say, and take a chair. Yes; there is something else I've got to say to you, and I want you to be frank with me."

Whatever it was that Mr. Wheatcroft had to say to Major Van Zandt it had to be said under the eyes of the clerks on the other side of the glass partition. And it took a long time saying, for it was evident to any observer of the two men as they sat in the private office that Mr. Wheatcroft was trying to force an explanation of some kind from the old book-keeper, and that the Major was resisting his employer's entreaties as best he could. Apparently the matter under discussion was of an importance so grave as to make Mr. Wheatcroft resolutely retain his self-control;

and not once did he let his voice break out explosively, as was his custom.

Major Van Zandt was still closeted with Wheatcroft when Mr. Whittier arrived. The senior partner stopped near the street door to speak to a clerk, and he was joined almost immediately by his son.

"Well, Paul," said the father, "have I got down here before you after all, and in spite of your running away last night ?"

"No," the son responded, "I was the first to arrive this morning—luckily."

" Luckily ?" echoed his father. "I suppose that means that you have been able to accomplish your purpose—whatever it was. You didn't tell me, you know."

" I'm ready to tell you now, father," said Paul, " since I have succeeded."

Walking down the store together, they came to the private office.

As the old book-keeper saw them he started up, and made as if to leave the office.

" Keep your seat, Major," cried Mr. Wheatcroft, sternly, but not unkindly. " Keep your seat, please."

Then he turned to Mr. Whittier. " I have

something to tell you both," he said, "and I want the Major here while I tell you.   Paul, may I trouble you to see that the door is closed so that we are out of hearing?"

"Certainly," Paul responded, as he closed the door.

"Well, Wheatcroft," Mr. Whittier said, "what is all this mystery of yours now?"

The junior partner swung around in his chair and faced Mr. Whittier.

"My mystery?" he cried.   "It's the mystery that puzzled us all, and I've solved it."

"What do you mean?" asked the senior partner.

"What I mean is, that somebody has been opening that safe there in the corner, and reading our private letter-book, and finding out what we were bidding on important contracts.   What I mean is, that this man has taken this information, filched from us, and sold it to our competitors, who were not too scrupulous to buy stolen goods!"

"We all suspected this, as you know," the elder Whittier said; "have you anything new to add to it now?"

"Haven't I?" returned Mr. Wheatcroft.
"I've found the man! That's all!"

"You, too?" ejaculated Paul.

"Who is he?" asked the senior partner.

"Wait a minute," Mr. Wheatcroft begged.
"Don't be in a hurry and I'll tell you. Yesterday afternoon, I don't know what possessed
me, but I felt drawn down-town for some
reason. I wanted to see if anything was
going on down here. I knew we had made
that bid Saturday, and I wondered if anybody
would try to get it on Sunday. So I came
down about four o'clock, and I saw a man
sneak out of the front door of this office. I
followed him as swiftly as I could and as
quietly, for I didn't want to give the alarm
until I knew more. The man did not see me
as he turned to go up the steps of the elevated
railroad station. At the corner I saw his face."

"Did you recognize him?" asked Mr. Whittier.

"Yes," was the answer. "And he did not
see me. There were tears rolling down his
cheeks, perhaps that's the reason. This morning I called him in here, and he has finally
confessed the whole thing."

"Who—who is it?" asked Mr. Whittier, dreading to look at the old book-keeper, who had been in the employ of the firm for thirty years and more.

"It is Major Van Zandt!" Mr. Wheatcroft declared.

There was a moment of silence; then the voice of Paul Whittier was heard, saying, "I think there is some mistake!"

"A mistake!" cried Mr. Wheatcroft. "What kind of a mistake?"

"A mistake as to the guilty man," responded Paul.

"Do you mean that the Major isn't guilty?" asked Mr. Wheatcroft.

"That's what I mean," Paul returned.

"But he has confessed," Mr. Wheatcroft retorted.

"I can't help that," was the response. "He isn't the man who opened that safe yesterday afternoon at half-past three and took out the letter-book." ·

The old book-keeper looked at the young man in frightened amazement.

"I have confessed it," he said, piteously—"I have confessed it."

"I know you have, Major," Paul declared, not unkindly. "And I don't know why you have, for you were not the man."

"And if the man who confesses is not the man who did it, who is?" asked Wheatcroft, sarcastically.

"I don't know who is, although I have my suspicions," said Paul; "but I have his photograph—taken in the act!"

V

WHEN Paul Whittier said he had a photograph of the mysterious enemy of the Ramapo Steel and Iron Works in the very act of opening the safe, Mr. Whittier and Mr. Wheatcroft looked at each other in amazement. Major Van Zandt stared at the young man with fear and shame struggling together in his face.

Without waiting to enjoy his triumph, Paul put his hand in his pocket and took out two squares of bluish paper.

"There," he said, as he handed one to his father, "there is a blue print of the man taken in this office at ten minutes past three yesterday afternoon, just as he was about to open the safe in the corner. You see he is kneeling with his hand on the lock, but apparently just then something alarmed him and he cast a hasty glance over his shoulder. At that second the photograph was taken, and so we have a full-face portrait of the man."

Mr. Whittier had looked at the photograph, and he now passed it to the impatient hand of the junior partner.

" You see, Mr. Wheatcroft," Paul continued, "that although the face in the photograph bears a certain family likeness to Major Van Zandt's, all the same that is not a portrait of the Major. The man who was here yesterday was a young man, a man young enough to be the Major's son !"

The old book-keeper looked at the speaker.

" Mr. Paul," he began, " you won't be hard on the—" then he paused abruptly.

" I confess I don't understand this at all !" declared Mr. Wheatcroft, irascibly.

" I am afraid that I do understand it," Mr. Whittier said, with a glance of compassion at the Major.

" There," Paul continued, handing his father a second azure square, "there is a photograph taken here ten minutes after the first, at 3.20 yesterday afternoon. That shows the safe open and the young man standing before it with the private letter-book in his hand. As his head is bent over the pages of the book, the view of the face is not so good. But there can be no doubt that it is the same man. You see that, don't you, Mr. Wheatcroft?"

"I see that, of course," returned Mr. Wheatcroft, forcibly. "What I don't see is why the Major here should confess if he isn't guilty!"

"I think I know the reason for that," said Mr. Whittier, gently.

"There haven't been two men at our books, have there?" asked Mr. Wheatcroft—"the Major, and also the fellow who has been photographed?"

Mr. Whittier looked at the book-keeper for a moment.

"Major," he said, with compassion in his voice, "you won't tell me that it was you who sold our secrets to our rivals? And you might confess it again and again, 1 should never believe it. I know you better. I have known you too long to believe any charge against your honesty, even if you bring it yourself. The real culprit, the man who is photographed here, is your son, isn't he? There is no use in your trying to conceal the truth now, and there is no need to attempt it, because we shall be lenient with him for your sake, Major."

There was a moment's silence, broken by Wheatcroft suddenly saying:

"The Major's son? Why, he's dead, isn't he? He was shot in a brawl after a spree somewhere out West two or three years ago —at least, that's what I understood at the time."

"It is what I wanted everybody to understand at the time," said the book-keeper, breaking silence at last. "But it wasn't so. The boy was shot, but he wasn't killed. I hoped that it would be a warning to him, and he would make a fresh start. Friends of mine got him a place in Mexico, but luck was against him—so he wrote me—and he lost that. Then an old comrade of mine gave him another chance out in Denver, and for a while he kept straight and did his work well. Then he broke down once more and he was discharged. For six months I did not know what had become of him. I've found out since that he was a tramp for weeks, and that he walked most of the way from Colorado to New York. This fall he turned up in the city, ragged, worn out, sick. I wanted to order him away, but I couldn't. I took him back and got him decent clothes and took him to look for a place, for I knew that hard work was the only thing that would keep him out of mischief. He did not find a place, perhaps he did not look for one. But all at once I discovered that he had money. He would not tell me how he got it. I knew he could not have come by it honestly, and so I watched him. I spied after him, and at last I found that he was selling you to the Tuxedo Company."

"But how could he open the safe?" cried Mr. Wheatcroft. "You didn't know the new combination."

"I did not tell him the combination I did know," said the old book-keeper, with pathetic dignity. "And I didn't have to tell him. He can open almost any safe without knowing the combination. How he does it, I don't know; it is his gift. He listens to the wheels as they turn, and he sets first one and then the other; and in ten minutes the safe is open."

"How could he get into the store?" Mr. Whittier inquired.

"He knew I had a key," responded the old book-keeper, "and he stole it from me. He used to watch on Sunday afternoons till Mike went for a walk, and then he unlocked the store, and slipped in and opened the safe. Two weeks ago Mike came back unexpectedly, and he had just time to get out of one of the rear windows of this office."

"Yes," Paul remarked, as the Major paused, "Mike told me that he found a window unfastened."

"I heard you asking about it," Major Van Zandt explained, "and I knew that if you were suspicious he was sure to be caught sooner or later. So I begged him not to try to injure you again. I offered him money to go away. But he refused my money; he said he could get it for himself now, and I might keep mine until he needed it. He gave me the slip yesterday afternoon. When I found he was gone I came here straight. The front door was unlocked; I walked in and found him just closing the safe here. I talked to him, and he refused to listen to me. I tried to get him to give up his idea, and he struck me. Then I left him, and I went out, seeing no one as I hurried home. That's when Mr. Wheatcroft followed me, I suppose. The boy never came back all night. I haven't seen him since; I don't know where

he is, but he is my son, after all—my only son!
And when Mr. Wheatcroft accused me, I confessed at last, thinking you might be easier on
me than you would be on the boy."

"My poor friend," said Mr. Whittier, sym-
pathetically, holding out his hand, which the
Major clasped gratefully for a moment.

"Now that we know who was selling us to
the Tuxedo people, we can protect ourselves
hereafter," declared Mr. Wheatcroft. "And
in spite of your trying to humbug me into be-
lieving you guilty, Major, I'm willing to let
your son off easy."

"I think I can get him a place where he will
be out of temptation, because he will be kept
hard at work always," said Paul.

The old book-keeper looked up as though
about to thank the young man, but there
seemed to be a lump in his throat which pre-
vented him from speaking.

Suddenly Mr. Wheatcroft began, explosively,
"That's all very well! but what I still don't understand is how Paul got those photographs!"

Mr. Whittier looked at his son and smiled.
"That is a little mysterious, Paul," he said,
"and I confess I'd like to know how you did it."

"Were you concealed here yourself?" asked Mr. Wheatcroft.

"No," Paul answered. "If you will look round this room you will see that there isn't a dark corner in which anybody could tuck himself."

"Then where was the photographer hidden?" Mr. Wheatcroft inquired, with increasing curiosity.

"In the clock," responded Paul.

"In the clock?" echoed Mr. Wheatcroft, greatly amazed. "Why, there isn't room in the case of that clock for a thin midget, let alone a man!"

Paul enjoyed puzzling his father's partner. "I didn't say I had a man there or a midget either," he explained. "I said that the photographer was in the clock—and I might have said that the clock itself was the photographer."

Mr. Wheatcroft threw up his hands in disgust. "Well," he cried, "if you want to go on mystifying us in this absurd way, go on as long as you like! But your father and I are entitled to some consideration, I think."

"I'm not mystifying you at all; the clock took the pictures automatically. I'll show you how," Paul returned, getting up from his chair and going to the corner of the office.

Taking a key from his pocket he opened the case of the clock and revealed a small photographic apparatus inside, with the tube of the objective opposite the round glass panel in the door of the case. At the bottom of the case was a small electrical battery, and on a small shelf over this was an electro-magnet.

"I begin to see how you did it," Mr. Whittier remarked. "I am not an expert in photography, Paul, and I'd like a full explanation. And make it as simple as you can."

"It's a very simple thing indeed," said the son. "One day while I was wondering how we could best catch the man who was getting at the books, that clock happened to strike, and somehow it reminded me that in our photographic society at college we had once suggested that it would be amusing to attach a detective camera to a timepiece and take snapshots every few minutes all through the day. I saw that this clock of ours faced the safe, and that it couldn't be better placed for the purpose. So when I had thought out my plan, I came over here and pretended that the clock was wrong, and in setting it right I broke off the minute-hand. Then I had a man I know send for it for repairs; he is both an electrician and an expert photographer. Together we worked out this device. Here is a small snap-shot camera loaded with a hundred and fifty films; and here is the electrical attachment which connects with the clock so as to take a photograph every ten minutes from eight in the morning to six at night. We arranged that the magnet should turn the spool of film after every snap-shot."

"Well!" cried Mr. Wheatcroft. "I don't know much about these things, but I read the papers, and I suppose you mean that the clock 'pressed the button,' and the electricity pulled the string."

"That's it precisely," the young man responded. "Of course I wasn't quite sure how it would work, so I thought I would try it first on a week-day when we were all here. It did work all right, and I made several interesting discoveries. I found that Mike smoked a pipe in this office — and that Bob played leap-frog in the store and stood on his head in the corner there up against the safe!"

"The confounded young rascal!" interrupted Mr. Wheatcroft.

Paul smiled as he continued. "I found also that Mr. Wheatcroft was captivated by a pretty book-agent and bought two bulky volumes he didn't want."

Mr. Wheatcroft looked sheepish for a moment.

"Oh, that's how you knew, is it?" he growled, running his hands impatiently through his shock of hair.

"That's how I knew," Paul replied. "I told you I had an eye on you. It was the lone eye of the camera. And on Sunday it kept watch for us here, winking every ten minutes. From eight o'clock in the morning to three in the afternoon it winked forty-two times, and all it saw was the same scene, the empty corner of the room here, with the safe in the shadow at first and at last in the full light that poured down from the glass roof over us. But a little after three a man came into the office and made ready to open the safe. At ten minutes past three the clock and the camera took his photograph—in the twinkling of an eye. At twenty minutes past three a second record was made.

Before half-past three the man was gone, and
the camera winked every ten minutes until
six o'clock quite in vain. I came down early
this morning and got the roll of negatives.
One after another I developed them, disappointed that I had almost counted fifty
of them without reward. But the forty-
third and the forty-fourth paid for all my
trouble."

Mr. Whittier gave his son a look of pride.
"That was very ingeniously worked out, Paul;
very ingeniously indeed," he said. "If it had
not been for your clock here I might have
found it difficult to prove that the Major was
innocent—especially since he declared himself
guilty."

Mr. Wheatcroft rose to his feet, to close the
conversation.

"I'm glad we know the truth, anyhow," he
asserted, emphatically. And then, as though
to relieve the strain on the old book-keeper, he
added, with a loud laugh at his own joke,
"That clock had its hands before its face all
the time—but it kept its eyes open for all
that!"

"Don't forget that it had only one eye,"

said Whittier, joining in the laugh; "it had an eye single to its duty."

"You know the French saying, father," added Paul, "'In the realm of the blind the one-eyed man is king.'"

(1895.)

A CONFIDENTIAL POSTSCRIPT

A CONFIDENTIAL POSTSCRIPT

T was pithily said by one of old that a bore is a man who insists upon talking about himself when you want to talk about yourself. There is some truth in the saying, no doubt; but surely it should not apply to the relation of an author to his readers. So long, at least, as they are holding his book in their hands, it is a fair inference that they do not wish to talk about themselves just that moment; indeed, it is not a violent hypothesis to suggest that perhaps they are then willing enough to have him talk about himself. For the egotistic garrulity of the author there is, in fact, no more fit occasion than in the final pages of his book. At that stage of the game he may fairly enough count on the good humor of his readers, since those who might be dissatisfied

with him would all have yielded to discourage-
ment long before the postscript was reached.

The customary preface is not so pleasant a
place for a confidential chat as the unconven-
tional postscript. The real value and the true
purpose of the preface is to serve as a tele-
phone for the writer of the book and to bear
his message to the professional book-reviewers. On the other hand, only truly devoted
readers will track the author to his lair in a
distant postscript. While it might be pre-
sumptious for him to talk about himself before
the unknown and anonymous book-reviewers,
he cannot but be rejoiced at the chance of a
gossip with his old friends, the gentle readers.

Perhaps the present author cannot drop into
conversation more easily than by here ventur-
ing upon the expression of a purely personal
feeling—his own enjoyment in the weaving of
the unsubstantial webs of improbable adventure that fill the preceding pages. With an
ironic satisfaction was it that a writer who is
not unaccustomed to be called a mere realist
here attempted fantasy, even though the results of his effort may reveal invention only
and not imagination. It may even be that it

was memory (mother of the muses) rather than invention (daughter of necessity) which inspired the ' Primer of Imaginary Geography.' I have an uneasy wonder whether I should ever have gone on this voyage of discovery with Mynheer Vanderdecken, past the Bohemia which is a desert country by the sea, if I had not in my youth been allowed to visit ' A Virtuoso's Collection'; and yet, to the best of my recollection, it was no recalling of Hawthorne's tale, but a casual glance at the Carte du Pays de Tendre in a volume of Molière, which first set me upon collecting the material for an imaginary geography.

In the second of these little fantasies the midnight wanderer saw certain combats famous in all literature and certain dances. Where it was possible use was made of the actual words of the great authors who had described these combats and these dances, the descriptions being condensed sometimes and sometimes their rhythm being a little modified so that they should not be out of keeping with the more pedestrian prose by which they were accompanied. Thus, as it happens, the dances of little Pearl and of Topsy could be set forth,

14

fortunately, almost in the very phrases of Hawthorne and of Mrs. Stowe, while I was forced to describe as best I could myself the gyrations of the wife who lived in 'A Doll's House' and of her remote predecessor as a "new woman," the daughter of Herodias. The same method was followed in the writing of the third of these tales, although the authors then drawn upon were most of them less well known; and the only quotation of any length was the one from Irving describing the mysterious deeds of the headless horseman.

Now it chanced that the 'Dream-Gown of the Japanese Ambassador,' instead of appearing complete in one number of a magazine, as the two earlier tales had done, was published in various daily newspapers in three instalments. In the first of these divisions the returned traveller fell asleep and saw himself in the crystal ball; in the second he went through the rest of his borrowed adventures; and in the third his friend awakened him and unravelled the mystery. When the second part appeared a clergyman who had read the 'Sketch-Book' (even though he had never heard of the 'Forty-Seven Ronins,' or the

'Shah-Nameh,' or the 'Custom of the Country') took his pen and sat down and wrote swiftly to a newspaper, declaring that this instalment of my tale had been "cribbed bodily, and almost *verbatim et literatim*, in one-third of its entire length, from the familiar 'Legend of Sleepy Hollow.'" He asked sarcastically if the copyright notice printed at the head of my story was meant to apply also to the passages plagiarized from Irving. He declared also that "it is unfortunate for literary persons of the stamp of the author of 'Vignettes of Manhattan' that there still exist readers who do not forget what they have read that is worth remembering. Such readers are not to be imposed on by the most skilful bunglers (*sic*) who endeavor to pass off as their own the work of greater men."

The writer of this letter had given his address, Christ Church Rectory, ———, N. J. (I suppress the name of the village for the sake of his parishioners as I suppress the name of the man for the sake of his family). Therefore I wrote to him at once, telling him that if he had read the third and final instalment of my story with the same attention he had given to the second part he would understand why I was expecting to receive from him an apology for the letter he had sent to the newspaper. In time there reached me this inadequate and disingenuous response, hardly worthy to be called even an apology for an apology:

"In reply to your courteous communication, let me say that had I seen the close of your short story, I should have grasped the situation more fully, and should doubtless have refrained from giving it any special attention.

"When one considers, however, the manner in which your copy was published by the paper, deferring the explanation until the appearance of the third instalment, it must be acknowledged that there was opportunity for surprise and criticism. The fault should have been found with the way in which the article was published, rather than with the story itself, that appearing at its conclusion a self-confessed mosaic of quotations. Needless to add that its author's aim to amuse, entertain, and instruct has been manifestly subserved.

"Yours most sincerely,

——— ———."

Of another tale ('Sixteen Years without a Birthday') I have nothing to say—except to record a friend's remark after he had finished it, that he had "read something very like it not long before in a newspaper;" so perhaps

I may be permitted to declare that I had not
read something very like it anywhere, but had,
to the best of my belief, " made it all up out
of my own head." Nor need I say anything
about the ' Rival Ghosts '—except to note that
it is here reprinted from an earlier collection
of stories which has now for years been out of
print.

The last tale of all, the ' Twinkling of an
Eye,' received the second prize for the best
detective story, offered by a newspaper syn-
dicate—the first prize being taken by a story
written by Miss Mary E. Wilkins and Mr. J. E.
Chamberlain. The use of the camera as a
detective agency had been suggested to me by
a brief newspaper paragraph glanced at casually several years before. And I confess that it
was with not a little amusement that I employed this device, since I had then recently
seen my ' Vignettes of Manhattan ' criticized as
being " photographic in method." Here again
I had no reason to doubt the originality of my
plot; and here once more was my confidence
shattered, and I was forced to confess that
fiction can never hope to keep ahead of fact.

After the ' Twinkling of an Eye ' was published in the newspapers which had joined in offering the prizes, it was printed again in one of the smaller magazines. There it was read by a gentleman connected with a hardware house in Grand Rapids, who wrote to me, informing me that the story I had laboriously pieced together had—in some of its details, at least—been anticipated by real life more than a year before I sat down to write out my narrative. This gentleman has now kindly given me permission to quote from his letter those passages which may be of interest to readers of the 'Twinkling of an Eye':

It appears that the cash-drawer of the hardware store, in which small change was habitually left over night for use in the morning before the banks open, was robbed three nights running, although only a few dollars were taken at a time. "The large vault, in which are kept the firm's papers, had not been tampered with, and the work was evidently that of some petty thief. The night-watchman was a trusted employee, and my father did not wish to accuse him unjustly. And, besides, he did not.wish to warn the thief. So nothing was said to the watchman. The nights on which the till had been tapped were Thursday, Friday, and Saturday. Father goes down to the store every Sunday morning for about half an hour to open the mail, and it was then that he discovered the Saturday night theft. Directly after Sunday dinner, father went down to see an electrical friend of his, who executed a plan which my father had devised. The cash-drawer was situated in one corner of the office (quite a large one), in which both the wholesale and retail business is transacted. He placed a large detective camera in the corner opposite the till, and beside it, and a little behind, a quantity of flash-light powder in a receptacle. This powder was connected by electric wires with the till in such a manner that when the drawer was opened the circuit would be completed and the powder ignited. Everything worked to perfection. The office is always left dark at night, so the shutter of the camera could be left open without spoiling the film. The camera was in place Sunday evening, but the thief stayed away. It was set again on Monday night, and that time we got him. A small wire was attached to a weight near the camera extending to the till. As the thief started to open the drawer the weight made a slight noise. He glanced in the direction of the noise, started, pulled the weight a little farther, and we had his picture. Detectives had already been working on the case, and the thief was identified and arrested on the strength of the portrait. When he was informed that we had his picture, he made a full confession. He said that when the flash-light went off he nearly fainted from fright."

After this experience I am tempted to give up all hope that I can ever invent anything which is not a fact, even before I make it up. I am now prepared, therefore, to discover that I did really have an interview with Count Cagliostro, and also that I was actually an unwilling witness at the wedding of the rival ghosts.

(1896.)

THE END